MW01222203

Dishonest Housekeepers

Dishonest Housekeepers

A Novella

HÉLÈNE ANDORRE HINSON STALEY

Copyright © 2007 by Hélène Andorre Hinson Staley and Metallo House Publishers.

International Standard Book Number (ISBN):   Softcover   978-1-4257-8707-3
Library of Congress Control Number (LCN):   2007903756

All rights reserved. No part of this book may be reproduced or transmitted in any form or by any means, electronic or mechanical, including photocopying, recording, or by any information storage and retrieval system, without permission in writing from the copyright owner.

This is a work of fiction. Names, characters, places and incidents either are the product of the author's imagination or are used fictitiously, and any resemblance to any actual persons, living or dead, events, or locales is entirely coincidental.

Dishonest Housekeepers, the short story version, the novella version and the screenplay adaptation are all artistic and creative expressions and works by the author. No part of *Dishonest Housekeepers* in any of its creative forms may be reproduced without the written and verbal permission of the author and publisher. No part of *Dishonest Housekeepers* is intended to offend any person, profession, culture, religion or country. It is the sole creative expression of the author.

This book was printed in the United States of America.

To order additional copies of this book, contact:
Xlibris Corporation
1-888-795-4274
www.Xlibris.com
Orders@Xlibris.com
28029

Table of Contents

A SPECIAL THANK YOU is extended to my son Zachary for his technical computer assistance and literary critiques. I thank my son Nicholas for his literary opinions and my son Benjamin for all the inspiration he provided during the writing process.

Dedication

TO MY SONS: Zachary, Nicholas & Benjamin in honor of their grandparents James and Patricia and great grandmothers: Virgie and Ruth, and great-great grandmother Susie.

MY PATERNAL GRANDMOTHER Virgie was the first person in my life to teach me about the dangers of snakes. During growing years, my maternal grandmother Ruth and maternal great grandmother Susie emphasized the importance of housekeeping.

THIS NOVELLA IS ALSO dedicated to my husband, Howard, a Doctor of Podiatric Medicine – commonly known as a podiatrist.

TRAVEL TO ANOTHER EXISTENCE, where clock faces gaze back when eyes stare too intently and snakes have much to do with unlocking clues.

Ella's on a journey to find an honest housekeeper – hoping to break a history of hiring and firing. Deception and greed are about to deliver dishonest housekeepers to a new employer and the estate overseer Edwin Hedgecroft.

Revelations about Ella's deepest fears and the deceptive practices of housekeepers make unexpected twisty turns that lead each character on a separate journey.

Introductive Thoughts

"Dreams are illustrations . . . from the book your soul is writing about you,"
Marsha Norman.

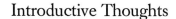

L OOK AT THE MOON, and you may briefly entertain yourself with chilling tales of wolves or old scarecrows frolicking with the wind amidst a gray-white glow in a field of Indian corn. Peer into another's dreams and memories, and you may find yourself quite at home.

YOU ARE ABOUT TO embark on a journey I hope will raise your spirits and souls to splendid heights of adventurous dreams.

Characters

Ella
Hal [Ella's husband]
Chris [Ella's eldest son]
Aaron [Ella's middle son]
Ethan [Ella's third son]
Mister Citrouilles [cat]
Housekeeper #1
Housekeeper #2
Housekeeper #3
Housekeeper #4
Housekeeper #5
Housekeeper #6
Daughter of Housekeeper #6
Housekeeper #7 [Trudare]
Housekeeper #8 [Billie-Barbara-Jean]
Housekeeper #9 [Catatina]
Housekeeper #10 [Lux Bux]
Mark Twain's spirit
William Miller's spirit
Wee Willie Winkie
Jesse [housekeeper]
Angie [prospect]
Miss V. Rae [Ella's confidante]
Soul
Spirit
Mr. Edwin Hedgecroft [butler & overseer of Irish estate]
Nameless female
Estate owner [man in dark clothes at the cemetery]
Horse [including the horse heads of two others]
Irish sheep farmer
Ella's father
Ella's brother John
Nameless stranger in Australia
A nun
Black snakes
Green snakes
Rattlesnake
King snake

Dishonest Housekeepers

Chapter 1

To Run With Ghosts

ANTICIPATION CAN steady nerves – but when we open the door to fear, our imagination can run as wild as a jaguar. The fog and breath that cloud air like puffs of smoke from a dragon's nares can take on new meaning. Quiet medieval woods of tawny brown-grays then hold in limbo the breaths and motions of the creature in pursuit of prey. It is fear more than curiosity that prompts us to ask – where and who is this prey? What is it we see exactly?

If we are angels or birds high on a perch, we see the cool-blue light. We see the gray sky peaking through a window below. We see the frozen glitz of crusty frost across a roof. We note the silence in the midst of gray shadows, cast from bushes and ivy vines.

Perhaps, if we are angels or old souls and spirits lounging the ghostly existence, we might see Ella. She wakes now as a shrieking eerie sound resonates into her ears and provokes prickles to stand on end the peach fuzz of her arms and neck. But what is this sound that prompts her to wake? It resembles possibly a hawk or bobcat. Ella sits up, waits and listens for the sound again, stands and slips on her shoes. Her walk outdoors transforms to running. Ella's feet pound the earth. Heartbeats, like a war cry, seem as loud as faceless sounds of a dark forest when we are afraid.

If we are indeed a bird on a perch, we certainly see the reaching crooked claw-like branches enveloping Ella like a giant's hand. Her constant motion is below us as dust rises from around her feet. Her breaths are bits of cloudy steam. Ella scurries desperately up a ladder to a hunter's loft. A jaguar pursues inches behind. If we are guardian angels, we buff the shock of the jaguar knocking Ella to the loft floor. Our hands hold her hands as she holds its face at bay. She falls with the creature as the loft crumbles to rubble.

Ella's face, dotted in dust, streams sweat in trails. The jaguar retreats. Within moments of this, another creature – a bear, confronts Ella. She runs. As angels are prone to influence, the bear changes its mind and retreats. The yellow-flames of morning rise in a starry-ball of orange glow through tree trunks and branches.

IT'S SEVEN O'CLOCK IN the morning. Ella writes at a well-worn, second-hand desk. She grasps a pen in one hand. The other hand presses pages of a journal flat. Ella's mind floats into the forest as it envelops her sense of being. She feels as if her study transforms into walls of trees. As she nears the end of her entry, she finds she is completely alone at her desk and walls of prints and photos. She writes:

"I run amidst the lost. The
unguided. I run with ghosts,
who fear judgment long after
severed cords stop fluttering
in the wind. Gathered in silver
strands toward the sun, they
slip into clouds. Pursuit sounds
behind. I run as the day raises
its yellow-tangerine flames.
I run until I wake up."

Ella closes her journal and places the pen next to it.

Chapter 2

No Negativity

IT IS 6:30 A.M. of the following day. Ella's mind again floats into the forest as it envelops her sense of being. Gray light finds its way through windows as bobwhites and other birds chirp faintly in the midst of luminous, peaceful solitude.

Ella opens her eyes. Her baby's cries are muted and low-key to the rest of the sleeping household. For Ella, the cries resonate into her ear canals, thoughts – into her soul and spirit – her inner core of existence. She stands and exits her bedroom to comfort her baby.

Neatly arranged in the sense of clutter, framed photos of Ella's family congregate the walls and dresser tops. Ella returns and walks to the window. This second-floor window overlooks the gravel drive and dry, waterless fountain-pond. A trio statue of smiling cherubs is turned toward the road. Ella cannot see their faces. They stand motionless in the pond amidst gray-blue morning light.

From the outside, Ella's bedroom window glows yellow as she prepares for the day. Like most, Ella spends at least one-third of life's complex circumstances and situations asleep. It seems strange the images of three cherubs of stone and metal are suspended in time – always awake in both realities of dreams and physical states of being. Of course, this can't possibly be! Their story, depicted by their play and frolic, is like some of those in Camille Claudel's sculptures, she supposes. Those seem so real. It is as if they might suddenly walk off and join the living.

Ella prepares to shower and dress. She scurries about searching for sandals. Upon finding them, she slides her perfected manicured feet into them. There are faint scars on the inside tops of her feet from bunionectomies. There are two small round scars on her right great toe from falling off a boat ramp. There is a fifth scar – a faint one, beneath her right ankle from an injury that required surgery.

Ella steps with a sixth sense around scattered toys on her way to the bathroom. There, she washes her face and brushes her teeth without turning on the light.

Steam fills the bathroom mirror like clouds rising from a forest stream at dusk. Ella makes a circle with her hand as one might wipe a dirty window.

"Another migraine walled off," she whispers.

"In thought, deed and without the verbalization of words and negativity."

Ella rinses and taps a toothbrush on the basin's side. Her eyes search her reflection as if directing another human soul. Then, she says,

"No negativity!"

Ella's manner is like one with unrestrained action to sing an unsolicited song on a public bus. The mirror steams again by warm, running water. Ella dries her face, walks from the bathroom, across the bedroom floor, and then stands in front of the nightstand. A journal rests there. She picks it up, opens a drawer, and retrieves a pen.

Ella writes as she continues standing. She rests the spine and journal's cover open against the inside fold of her left arm, and writes:

> *"My spirit is a purple soldier*
> *without a sword. It stomps a*
> *noisy march. It distracts*
> *judgments. It pours bright*
> *light into my soul as I sleep.*
> *The door to me swings open. My*
> *soul jumps out. It bumps my*

spirit. It says not the least,
'Excuse me,' or 'Where have you
been?' It just seems to know
something I do not."

Ella places her journal on the nightstand, gathers clothing items from drawers, walks toward her closet, and mumbles:

"At best, do something – write something other than journal notes!"

She shuffles about, gathers her robe and returns to the bathroom. She ponders inventions – those she put to paper. She wonders if one might end the need for gasoline and oil.

Ella steps into the shower, shampoos her hair and rinses her face.

"A car with pedals like a bicycle – the only thing a battery is used for is directed toward windshield wipers, lights, signals," she says.

"Perhaps, with solar panels. A baby bathtub that incorporates into a regular bathtub; a baby-in-vehicle alarm, a child-proof plastic cactus dome."

Chapter 3

What We're Made of

ELLA STANDS ON THE right side porch of her home. Birds chirp. Other morning forest-type sounds resonate the air. Ella hands a stack of invention ideas with detailed descriptions and drawings to her husband Hal.

Hal sits in a porch chair, resting his right foot on the opposite knee. His elongated toenails look more like rough and wild fingernails – similar – if not worse, an older Howard Hughes style. He sports open-toed sandals as he grasps the papers, glances through them and places them on a nearby table. He hums, pauses in thought, hums again, breathes a deep breath and exhales. He lights a cigarette, inhales, holds the smoke, and then blows it sideways.

"Do you think better smoking those?" Ella asks.

Hal removes a tissue from a pocket and wipes his glasses.

"No, not really," he says.

"No. Not at all. Quitting is a well-traveled road. It's a traffic jam of good intentions. Isn't it?"

Ella steps closer.

"Like tending to those?" she asks.

She glances Hal's feet. His eyes stare intently at her. As he lowers his glance, he crushes a cigarette into a bucket of sand, ignoring Ella's reference to his toenails.

"I can't say I'm thrilled about most of these inventions," he says.

"But, they are certainly unique."

Hal stands, walks across the porch singing quietly to himself, and then looks through screened-in windows into the yard. A cat sleeps on a lawn chair.

"Oh, let me sleep on it," Hal mumbles.

"Let me sleep on it. I will give you an answer in the morning . . . or the afternoon."

Ella looks about the porch as if concerned for something outside of her conversation with Hal.

"Are you just impatient or unimaginative?" she asks.

"These inventions are close to my heart. When I create anything, it's a reflection of what I'm made of. What are you made of?"

Hal looks around, scratches the beardy stubble of his chin, takes a deep breath and responds playfully nearly whispering:

"Are you speaking to me? I mean, of course, you are speaking to me . . . Toenails?"

Ella glances the look of *you-know-who* I'm talking to. Hal gazes Ella's face. Then, he looks out the screened-in window toward the cat Mister Citrouilles.

"Sometimes, you know," Hal hesitates.

"You talk with our cats. Do you fancy them human?" he asks.

"One more thing. You are forever, mumbling in your sleep."

Ella closes her eyes briefly then opens them.

"This is not an invitation to fight," she replies.

"If you want to do that, join the military."

As Hal clears his throat, he pats his shirt pocket for cigarettes. Ella looks upward; sighs quietly.

"I like the baby bathtub idea, by the way," Hal says.

He lights another cigarette. Ella steps back to avoid smoke. She gazes with renewed interest as if this time Hal might supply encouraging feedback.

"Thank you," she says.

"But I believe you are avoiding my question."

Hal takes a deep breath, exhales, turns his attentions upward, then asks:

"On good days? Let me see."

He hesitates, then adds:

"Bunionectomies, heel spur and ankle surgeries. On really great days, payment for these things."

Hal smiles, chuckles, glances upward, gazes Ella's face and then peers through the window. The cat distracts him.

"What about on bad days?" Ella asks.

Hal turns his visual focus off of the cat and onto Ella.

"Wait a moment," he says.

"I'm not there yet. On so-so days. Let me see."

Hal pauses, takes a deep breath, holds it, exhales slowly and looks at Ella.

"Ingrown toenails and pus pockets," he continues.

Ella takes an amused tone.

"What about fungus and warts?" she asks.

Hal scratches his chin.

"Fungus and warts?" he asks.

"That's what I use to throw at people who don't pay their bills," he replies.

Ella unties the back of her apron and tosses it across her right arm.

"Oh, get on with it," she says.

"Tell me, what are you made of?"

Hal puckers his lips, closes his eyes as if deep in thought, then lets go of the pucker and says:

"On bad days . . . a cigarette's rage.   No, on bad days, I take a callous approach; accepting no corn from bogus insurance companies . . . or drug addicts seeking to use me to abuse themselves. I become Doctor Hype. Yes. Doctor Hype. You know his associate, Doctor Heckle very well? I say, 'I enjoyed your little show; now find your way to the door, and take all your little donkeys and wolves with you.' Then, I eat the lunch I forgot on my desk the day before and accidentally step on the new one.   I come home and throw up what is seeking to become a part of me."

Ella looks away, then asks:

"No snakes or puppy dog tails?"

Hal answers,

"What are you made of?"

[A sign posted by the porch door states:
"NO SMOKING PAST THIS DOOR."]

Ella does not reply. She opens the screen door and walks inside the house to the kitchen. Her journal rests on the counter. She opens it and writes:

"Dreams. I'm made of dreams!
Constant sleep deprivation.
Ninety percent water. Ten
percent breast milk. Fifty
tons in the wee morning. I
run from bears. I battle
jaguars. Now, who needs coffee
and cream?"

Ella sighs, breathes out and resumes writing:

"Prudes are annoyed;
uncomfortable with breast
milk. They squirm. They
twist in pompous piety.
Their faces shout: 'It's
unnatural.' It's delegated
to lower animals. Cheers
to breast milk."

Ella lifts a glass of orange juice and takes a sip.

"For breakfast, lunch and dinner," she says to herself.

"God bless the milk. Blessed cheers. How about some milk with that?"

Ella places her pen down, pours coffee into a cup decorated with feet and leaves it on the counter for Hal. She walks to her son Ethan, where he rests in a carrier. Ella picks him up. He is a bundle of beauty. He nurses. His curls are in a delicate noggin of shiny blond ringlets that accent his soft-blue eyes and porcelain face.

"When you sleep, you live in my soul," Ella says to Ethan.

"You get to see some of my dream adventures; don't you? You are a little papoose then. Right?"

Ethan rests against Ella's arm and snuggles contently. Ella pulls him closer.

"You and your brothers are the love of my life – my absolute reason," she whispers.

"*I battle and run from bears and jaguars. The snakes? We need to face them head on. Right? Absolutely, yes. Yes, indeed. Let's not forget. One day, we will send them packing. What an adventure! They won't soon forget it, now will they?*"

Chapter 4

One Afternoon

IT IS 4 P.M. – sunny with clear-blue skies. Ella drives to the public library through winding curves and slopes. Her two eldest sons Chris and Aaron wait on an outdoor bench. They greet Ella with kisses and place their book bags into the Jeep™. During the drive home, Ella stops momentarily to allow a black snake to finish its journey crossing the road.

Later, Ella stands in front of the sink, glances the wall clock, and reads: *"4:30 p.m."* Ella's hands redden as she washes vegetables. She does this and other household chores when she hears Aaron screaming for help from another room,

"Save me Mom!"

Aaron runs as his elder brother Chris pursues him with a fly swatter. The eldest runs past nearly bumping into Ella.

"What do you recall about running?" she asks.

"Not in the house! Leave your brother be. Do your chores. Take a shower. Do your homework. Not a word."

Chris clutches the handle of the fly swatter.

"Are you not going to defend me?" he asks.

Ella places one hand at her waist and looks directly into Chris's eyes. With the opposite hand, she moves her son's chin upward. Chris glances away.

"You are the one with the fly swatter," Ella says.

"Why should I defend you?"

Chris gazes at her in exasperation.

"Then, here," he says.

"You take it. Use it."

"If I were you, I would re-think that suggestion, and put it where I can't find it," Ella responds.

Chris walks to the stairs and goes to his room. Aaron peeks from an opposite doorway and steps out of hiding.

"Mommy . . . Thank you for saving me," he says.

Ella bites her lower lip momentarily.

"Get going before I change my mind," she replies.

Aaron secures a fast kiss and scampers off.

A thunderstorm vibrates and shakes floors and windows. Ella stops what she is doing, observes the walls, walks into the foyé, opens the door and looks through the porch and into the sky. There are no clouds – no drops of rain. She closes the door, and as she does, thunder rattles the ceiling. It is louder and followed by indiscernible shrieking high-pitched sounds.

"Mommy! Help me! Save me Mommy!" Chris yells suddenly.

Ella looks down at the floor, then upward, gazes the top of the stairwell and demands in a clear voice:

"Stop fighting. Get yourselves to separate rooms. Now!"

Like a herd of buffalo, Chris and Aaron race through upstairs rooms to the top of the stairs. This time Aaron chases Chris with a toy fishing rod. Ella stares at the top of the stairwell. One son pursues the other then passes out of sight. Ella pats perspiration from her forehead, upper lip and neck just before exclaiming in exasperation:

"Put that back where it belongs. Stop running. Stop fighting. Stop scarring my walls!"

Hours pass as the previous sibling battle does. The house grows quiet, and Ella resumes her household duties. She washes stray glasses and dishes, then dries her hands on a dishtowel. She places her watch, which now reads: *"7 p.m.,"* onto her wrist.

The two eldest sons are best buddies now. The acid in Ella's stomach is howling out from Barmy Town for a gallon of water and a package of antacids.

For Ella, who left newspapers 16 years earlier and later, a technical writing and editing position for an international computer company, life has gone through a metamorphosis of daily runs through her home. Up and down stairs she travels from one task to the next, often doing laundry with a baby on one hip, a pot of soup cooking, and a cake baking.

Ella strides through her home picking up discarded socks, shoes, book bags, candy wrappers and things she dare not identify – spit balls of paper, sticky paper airplanes and bottle caps. Ella retreats to the kitchen, scrubs countertops, and in barely audible words, says:

"We need a housekeeper. I don't want strangers intruding upon my privacy, but I need assistance."

Ella glances her knees and rubs them.

"Oh, my knees and back!" she says.

"Get some help! If I don't look out for myself, who will?"

Chapter 5

Home Life

Eight months later . . .

OFFICE WALLS AND BOOK-CASES and other furnishing are cluttered with the history of Ella's former career writing for newspapers. The wind blows and whistles through tiny household crevices. Ella walks out of her office and begins descending stairs through the garage, then walks through a breezeway, to a side porch, and then through the kitchen door. Ella's ankles are sockless and turn pink as she walks through December temperatures. She carries Ethan close to her chest.

She has been at the desk conducting her regular regime: genealogical research, notes, an occasional letter or poem. She walks to the kitchen. Hal enters from another room as Ella steps into the house.

"Have you seen my glasses?" he asks.

Ella responds matter-of-factly,

"They are on your head."

"Thank you," he replies.

"Two questions. Where is the power bill?"

Ella points to the magnetic clip on the refrigerator door.

"It's right there," she says.

"It's in front of you. See it?"

Ella looks at Hal and later about the floor and walls and back again.

"Another question?" she asks in an annoyed tone.

"Sometimes I'm undervalued. Clean underpants, socks, towels, bar of soap, napkin anyone? Perhaps a toothpick? I just live for this. What's your question? Is it on world peace? The hungry or poor? The war in Iraq? George W. Bush? No? Better? Maybe, a spider has taken residence in the bathtub? You need me to retrieve it? Oh, George Bush is in the bathtub? You need bug spray?"

Hal shakes his head.

"No. No. No. None of that," he says.

"Where are the antacids? I thought maybe you would like to go out for Mexican food later?"

Standing against the counter and tilting her head downward, Ella closes her eyes in search of inner peace.

"You know I detest eating out; unless we have no choice," she says.

"I inevitably find a hair or two in our food, or I catch sight of the cook with his finger up his nose, or the waiter scratching his bum with an order pad."

Ella's face is pleasant. Emotionless, but drained. She looks on and smiles.

"Yes," she adds.

"That spoils appetites," Hal says.

"We will be careful. No restaurants with butt-scratching waiters, nose-picking cooks or hair-shedding employees."

Ella breathes as if a tiny bit relieved.

"You take the boys out," she says.

"I'll stay here with Ethan and nap."

Ella walks to the oven, removes a cake cooling in a pan and turns it onto a plate. It breaks through the middle. She plasters it with frosting, then dusts the top with cinnamon. As she repairs the damage, Ella's flushed face turns toward the antacids in clear view on the counter. Chris walks into the kitchen.

"Is that cake for us or someone else?" he asks.

Ella pushes a strand of hair from her eyes.

"For dessert later today, after lunch or dinner and after you return home," she says.

"Not before you brush those teeth for the first time today. So go along. Get that done. Will you?"

Chapter 6

A Mother's Work is Never Done

WINTER BLOWS ITS COLDNESS through any available crevice and crack of Ella's home. She walks into the kitchen and discovers a plate of crumbs. The cake is gone.

"Glad to see you enjoyed it," Ella says quietly to herself.

She wipes frosting off of the counter and gazes at the empty cake plate.

As the day wanes on, Ella finds her work approaches a resting point. She shuts down the computer, stands in front of her desk and walks to the door. She strides into the house to the baby's nursery. Around her neck is a locket-watch. She grasps it as she opens the back to view a miniature photo of her children and checks the time. It's *"2 a.m."* Ella turns her attentions to the baby.

"I'm completely in Your hands," she says.

"The hands You gave me are going to fill a vaporizer and change a diaper of we-know-what," Ella says as if in prayer.

Ella reads most popular bestsellers on how to organize children's lives – how to keep the household healthy, happy. She walks into a bathroom and notices the seat up.

"I wish just for once males would recollect to put the seat down," she mumbles.

Chapter 7

A Rare Flower

TWO AND A HALF HOURS later at precisely 4:30 a.m. December winds blow over Ella's house. The temperatures inside the house dip causing Ella to wake. She sluggishly strides to the bathroom. She sits down and falls into the toilet.

"For the love of!" she exclaims.

Water splashes. No one wakes. The cats alert slightly. Ella walks to her bedroom, climbs into bed, then closes her eyes.

Later during the day, Ella enters her son Aaron's room. The walls here are decorated in moons and stars. Ella notices an unusual and offensive odor, follows the odor to a closet door, and turns the knob.

In a book bag, she discovers and counts 15 bagged ancient, blue fungus hair-growing school lunch sandwiches. Repulsion and shock show in Ella's face. She walks about her home – retrieving discarded clothes like a slave on a mission to escape.

"Harmony? The neighbor's donkey is harmonious!" Ella's mind shouts to itself.

"There's nothing harmonious playing referee. Taunting and revenge. Nothing harmonious. A sea of laundry, plastered dishes, sticky floors.

"To write in the midst of hell, chaos, rebellion [that is the question.] Not a related soul brave enough to ask: 'Let me help you?'

"Excuses abound. They have their lives; problems to tackle. Yes. A housekeeper. It's the answer. What? Travel this road? Again? How can you? Housekeepers! They manage to leave. Lurchy lurches! They are the greatest King Kong images. Cumulonimbus clouds, they are!"

Ella, surprised, discerns a dusty cloud of talc powder rising from the floor as she strides through. Following the trail, she discovers an empty talc container. She squats to the floor, stands again, retrieves a vacuum and cleans it up as the fog dissipates.

Housekeepers, Ella surmises, wait. They are wild cats ready to pounce. They are an endless sea. Oodles get washed ashore. This sea shares its waters with reprobates, degenerates, misdirected and lost souls.

[At this point in this story, you might assume it's up to Ella to fish them out – to weed out the jellyfish – scoop them and throw them into obscurity, the unknown?]

As Ella opens a closet door to retrieve the vacuum nearby, she imagines discerning a masquerader from a bonafide housekeeper.

"Well, thank you for taking time to interview," she says.

"I will let you know if we need you. Good-bye. Good luck. Bon voyage! Go-way!"

Ella whispers resentfully, and then puts the vacuum into a closet.

"No matter what the outcome," she says.

"There is always karma. What goes around, comes around."

Ella walks about her home's interior.

Ella moves through a string of Mommy-duties and cleans and works with the skill of an acrobat. Working at the computer and nursing is a skill Ella has perfected. Changing a diaper, answering the phone, cooking and refereeing simultaneously are part of her job description too. She promises the next venture for finding household help will not disappoint; unless the housekeeper should be great and just quit.

"Look for potential," she says.

Ella looks at her checkbook, considers the household's budget and extras her children manage to get past her: Too many Gameboy® games, Nintendo® games, computer games, Pokémon® cards, and seemingly meaningless collectibles. Extra candies and cookies. Trips to play golf while forgetting to clean their rooms and empty the garbage.

Ella can stop extras and hire extra. The possibility of hiring a housekeeper moves from luxury to necessity. Days pass until Ella finds herself alone in the house with her youngest child napping. She is still without a housekeeper. She sits, stretches across a queen-sized bed and crawls into one of Mark Twain's short stories, briefly interrupting to glance the clock radio, which reads: *"2 p.m."*

Ella's eyes feel heavy when suddenly, a voice is heard. To any well-read Southerner, the voice is that of Mark Twain – also known as Samuel Langhorne Clemens, born November 30th, 1835 in Florida, Missouri; died April 21st, 1910 in Redding (Stormfield), Connecticut.

"Welcome aboard," the voice says.

"How do you do?"

Because it is reasonable to conclude Twain is in fact beyond the physical state of the living – we must assume the voice Ella hears is that of his spirit. Ella's state-of-mind, however, although concerned, is exhausted. When exhaustion is part of any formula for sleep – except where a crying baby or child is of the utmost, concern takes a second seat.

Still, Ella believes she hears someone speaking. She imagines Twain's spirit. Her eyes close as she grasps the book, takes hold of Twain's hand, lets go, opens the book and drifts to sleep before reading more than the title and the first sentence.

"Come on now," the voice of Twain continues.

"Walk inside. Visit a while. Put your feet up. Adjust the pillows. Relax. Go ahead. Take a deep breath. Stay a spell."

Ella breathes a deep sigh as she reads the title.

"Was it Heaven or Hell?"

Ella's mind begins to ponder.

"Was it Heaven or Hell?"

Twain's spirit calls to Ella, as he desires to provide clues. His story regards a subject Ella is frequently on the receiving end of: Liars. Twain's transparent Spirit, clothed in his typical white suit, sports a white mustache. He crosses one leg over the other. As Ella sleeps, she believes she reads. She slips; however, further into this dream.

"Is this fate?" Twain's spirit asks Ella.

"You might imagine it is."

Twain smiles contently as Ella reads. Ella does not look back at him. Twain's story concerns two old maids. Their sainthood stance is to never lie. They discover lying to a sick niece and grandniece is necessary. Both die without knowing the other is near death.

They learn insistence for truth exposes an innocent to illness. They come to believe going to Hell is a sacrifice. They are asked:

"Was it heaven or hell?"

Ella mulls through ways people lie. Some live lies. Direct lies. Implied lies. Wordless lies. Assumption lies. Naturally, Ella's not a saint.

Ella might lie to an ill-intended stranger to gain ground, or to save life, or to stop persecution. She might lie to a telemarketer, or allow another to assume a lie when rebuttal is viewed as guilt.

Ella shuts the book, places it on the nightstand, leans back and closes her eyes. At 3 p.m., Ella opens her eyes and sits up. She is *officially* awake now.

"This is a rare flower that blooms only in the purest of conditions," she says to herself.

"A rare flower indeed!" Twain's spirit whispers angrily.

Ella looks about as if she heard someone other than herself. Just below Ella's bedroom is the garden, full of spiked and barbed devil's weed. A snake slithers through the neglected rows of bloomless roses. Ella takes an aspirin, downs a gulp of water from a glass on the nightstand, glances a window, re-opens the book and reads.

The clock ticks away the hours. At 1 a.m., Ella is deep in slumber. And while she rests, her Soul, dressed in a loud and brightly colored Hawaiian shirt, shorts, a Bahamian straw hat, over-sized sunglasses, water sandals, and a camera around his neck, emerges with hope of entering the spiritual realm.

Its companion Spirit, dressed in a long nightshirt and nightcap, holds a lit candle like Jack Be Nimble or Wee Willie Winkie. Both stand in Ella's room. They pace and glance the night sky through a window while waiting for Ella to drift deeper into sleep.

Spirit and Soul are two separate entities – yet they are part of Ella's existence. Their images are slightly transparent. They are never seen or heard by Ella. Surprisingly, they are both male.

Soul looks about the bedroom before directing his complete attention to Spirit.

"It's not easy being one's soul," he says.

"You suggest my job as spirit and general caretaker is easier?" Spirit replies.

Soul, not replying directly to this question, pauses as if in deep thought.

"You stay here," he says, as his face shines with an idea.

"Wait for me."

Spirit sighs.

"That's no deal," he answers.

"You know it. If you go, I will have to follow. That's not in the plan. Hold the horses. This is not the Apocalypse. There are no horsemen here! No Armageddon. Not for a long while."

Spirit refocuses his attentions.

"We should not wake her too soon," he says.

"There's the danger she might remember this dream and our conversation."

Soul and Spirit sit at the foot of Ella's bed and converse unheard. They converse in a manner of children at a slumber party or those gathered around a campfire. Soul and Spirit say more on future naps and snoozes. They just can't stop talking like two entities with Attention Deficit Disorder. They alternate being focused, then bombarded with concerns, unable to focus. It's a wonder Ella sleeps at all.

As Ella sleeps, Soul and Spirit continue to converse. Soul scratches his head and removes his sunglasses.

"The energies comprised in Ella rest in us," he says.

"If she perishes, we must find another occupation. I'm not prepared for what that might mean."

Spirit removes his nightcap and pours a glass of water. Soul changes his shirt to a white tunic. He pulls the visible tunic out of an invisible closet, shakes it like a little rug and puts it on.

Spirit takes a sip of water.

"Yes," he says.

"I would hate to feel the fullest of what her outrage might come to. She must find a way to balance negativity that occupies her world. Her life should not be a place Hades should visit."

Soul buttons the tunic as if somewhat aggravated.

"Oh, and would you assume she should find it later?" he asks.

Spirit wipes his mouth with a napkin after gulping down the rest of his water.

"Of course, not," he says.

"Indeed no. Absolutely no! Have you lost your mind?"

Soul and Spirit pause to check their sleeping human creature. Soul nudges her cheek to make sure she's okay – that her mind is there. Then, she nearly wakes.

"Wait!" Spirit shouts.

"What are you doing? What are you trying to do? Get us all three into trouble?"

Spirit and Soul agree. Ella's mind might become bogged. Such consequences could land them into lower levels. Lower levels would transport them to the holding place for the spiritually and soulfully wounded.

On the spiritual side of existence, the holding place is a dark castle bordered by oceans of steamy hot waters. On the human side, it's the state mental hospital.

Soul pauses a moment as he imagines such images – a creepy castle. It is surrounded by hot steamy waters. Alligators swim and snap about. Then, he imagines the façade of the state mental hospital. Apprehensively, Soul, in his imagined nightmare, knocks at the front door. Someone on the other side knocks back. This continues three or four times until Soul fearfully runs off.

Spirit pauses a moment as he imagines another image – a hospital surrounded in cloudy-gassy waters. His daydream includes Twain waiting at the entrance. He holds a bucket of whitewash and a paintbrush.

"A rare flower indeed!" Twain shouts.

"Now, get to work."

Twain's suit pants are rolled at the cuff three inches above his ankles. His feet are long and narrow with notable bunions and hammer toes. Such nightmare-like daydreams blink away as both Soul and Spirit begin to have some serious worries about their sleeping earthly entity.

"She can't do this on her own," Soul says.

Spirit, holding a rosary in one hand and a scrub brush in the other, says:

"We can pray about this. Yes. We can consult Mother and Father Nature. We can scrub away bad karma. What do you say?"

Soul adjusts his clothing.

"Ella is certainly as stressed as are we," Soul responds.

"Her current imbalance tilts our world like a seesaw with the son of The Addams Family Pugslie on one end and The Good Ship Lollypop on the other."

Chapter 8

Waiting

THE WINTER SKY IS a gray-cream, pearly haze. Ella glances from a window, yawns, tires and desires a nap as she waits for housekeeping prospects to arrive. A car door closes. Seconds later, the clacking of shoes is against the pathway.

A woman's feet, adorned in sensible shoes, stride the pathway. A hand lifts the knocker. Sound bounces against the walkway like decisive steps across a basketball court. It dissolves to fainting echoes.

The newcomer waits as she glances behind through damp limbs and foliage. Squirrels, birds and rabbits dot moist grass and leaves. Clouds turn dark.

The prospect steps closer to the doorway to shield her body from impending rain. Dust washes away into streams and ditches. A dry wind blows. Puddles and raindrops dry and disappear. Thick, gray dust from a brush fire on its way out makes its way across the sky like an anxious spirit. Its smudge settles against windows. Ella notices, then yawns.

Soul stretches and yawns.

"Where are the dreams of yesteryear?" he asks.

Spirit's manner approaches near sarcasm.

"And the fanciful dreams of today and for seasons to come?" he inquires.

"Stop talking like that."

Soul and Spirit stand glancing out a window. They are located several feet from Ella who pushes tresses from her eyes. Again, I emphasize, she is never conscious or aware of Soul and Spirit or their conversations. Ella stands in front of a window looking into dogwoods, pines, oaks, maples and whatever other trees one can imagine.

A cluster of daffodils grows outside the window. The doorbell rings. Ella walks to a mirror – checks her face and teeth briefly, then opens the door.

"Hello. I'm Angie."

Ella replies,

"Come in, please."

Ella escorts the prospect to the living room. Ella's eyes widen as her mouth curls into a nervous grin. She swallows as she is distracted by Angie's large gold tooth, two buns atop her head on both sides and long black-painted fingernails. Everything else seems within normal limits.

Ella thinks to herself, in the detailed manner she is accustomed to do.

"Why is it every prospect greets with smiles that mouth the words: 'Yes, mam. Why, I love to sweep and scrub floors. My favorite thing to do is to clean toilets.'"

At a window, Spirit and Soul stand observing Ella.

"I was nearly stretched out enough for a nap – but no, this had to be," Soul says.

"I need a reprieve. Ella needs a nap. Now, I listen to Ella reminisce on toilets? Where are those horses? I could beg for them now!"

Spirit looks into a mirror that reveals not the slightest reflection.

"I told you before. This is not the Apocalypse," he says.

Soul observes the prospects feet.

"Well, it could very well be," he says.

"Look at this prospect – a demon in disguise! Who does it think it's fooling?"

Spirit gazes at Soul with keener interest.

"Will you so kindly close your mouth?" he asks.

"Ella has better sense than to hire her. Relax."

Angie walks in. A small herd of transparent unsightly demons and vipers follow. Angie and Ella are not privy to seeing them. Soul and Spirit notice immediately and look away in disgust. Ella's smile hides true thoughts.

"None ever say, for example: 'This is how I survive," she says to herself.

"It is what I am qualified to do – not necessarily what I want, what anyone wants for a living, really. It's just my lot. I will do my best to meet the job's requirements!"

Soul sighs as if aggravated.

"Yes," he says.

"Let's meet requirements so I can go on a tiny vacation. We need to discover what the future holds. Consult hope and the guardian angels – not another toothy prospect. In particular, the angel with the scissors is looking very good about now. Ahh!"

Spirit gazes the ceiling, then turns his eyes to the floor and taps his heels.

"I asked politely," he says with hindered aggravation.

"Now, I'm telling you. You will not get a nap. I will make sure of it! The angel of death is not waiting with scissors. She is not going to cut our cord for several decades. Close your mouth, please."

Unfortunately, some of the Spirit's reply spills over into Ella's thoughts. It begins flowing from Ella's mouth – in particular, the part about a nap.

"A nap would be nice," Ella says to herself.

"Oh, now you have done it!" Soul shouts at Spirit.

Angie greedily turns her focus from various tabletop treasures completely to Ella.

"I'm sorry," she says.

"Is this a bad time?"

"No. It's the perfect time," Ella replies.

Angie smiles as she looks about the room, then focuses on Ella. Ella's mind swims in thought. No doubt the only ones who hear her private thoughts are Soul and Spirit, when she thinks:

"I doubt any are truly in love with this sort of work. If I manage to find one – a normal one, she will be a godsend. A rarely-to-never possibility. It might even be the dream of all dreams."

Ella yawns.

"It's fanciful thinking to believe anyone will ever take pleasure in this work," Ella thinks to herself.

"Placing their faces and hands into household caves and cavities and polishing them."

The interview process continues. Ella's mind fills with a hodgepodge of past hired domestic help – most leave spiked footprints across her back. As Ella ponders such, and seemingly listens to Angie, Soul and Spirit travel to Memory Lane with Ella.

Spirit and Soul join hands and smile sarcasm at one another as if ready to skip down the Yellow Brick Road. But the Yellow Brick Road is not on Memory Lane. It's definitely not here. Nevertheless, Soul is dressed like Little Boy Blue and Spirit as Jack Be Quick. Spirit stands next to a street sign that reads:

"Memory Lane."

He grasps his left hand around the street pole.

"Stop watching that clock," he says to Soul.

Angie is unaware of the conversation between Soul and Spirit.

"I'm sorry," Angie says.

"Did you say something about clocks?"

Surprised, Ella asks,

"No. Did I?"

The prospect resumes her journey of trying to convince Ella of her skilled knowledge.

Chapter 9

The Prospects of Memory Lane

E LLA'S MIND FILLS WITH memories that take her to a place all humans and other animals alike know as *"Memory Lane."* In fact, this place is so well known, its main street is named for it.

The street may look differently from one person's mind to the next, but town governments of such places also eventually erect street signs when traveled there often enough. It's not that the person or people traveling there can't recall how to get around. The signs serve as healthy reminders that prompt each person to ask:

"Do I really want to go this route again?"

Of course, when memories become shared experiences, *overlap* results, and people from our pasts find themselves congregating on the same street. It can get a bit crowded. The mayor of such a place must find some way to keep the streets – particularly *"Memory Lane"* organized.

The one in Ella's mind looks like something out of a Mother Goose tale on a dark, misty gothic backdrop. The gothic background evolves over a long period of time when the mayor of this place discovers Memory Lane's visitors share a lot in common. Most all of them have histories of taking unfair advantage over Ella's good nature, yes, but very often they took advantage of her insecurities.

Some may know that Mother Goose tales have deeper meanings than those ascribed to them by young children and their parents. In Ella's mind, the symbolism of Humpty Dumpty, for example, was more than just a 15th century colloquial term reserved for the greatly obese, or even the large cannon used during the English Civil War (1642-1649) – a war between Royalists and Parliamentarians or Roundheads. To Ella, Humpty Dumpty was in fact a giant egg of a former housekeeper who rolled over her back leaving egg not only on Ella's face – but all over her body and house. And every time she thought of this housekeeper, she saw her house in Memory Lane dripping in gallons of raw egg.

In Ella's mind, the symbolism of Wee Willie Winkie went beyond this character being the town crier passing on the latest information and news. On Memory Lane she sees Winkie's author William Miller (1810-1872) on the sidelines like a sort of modern-day counselor trying to break through the loss of self. They are very much like such walls dishonest housekeepers construct.

For such barriers are often made like iron and steel or splinter-ridden wood with rusty nails and bolts. They evolve, as the best of psychiatrists know because the parents and caretakers of such individuals during childhood never mirrored their truest feelings and concerns. Their selfish motives overlooked their innocence and drove out the good that humans are born with and replaced it with lies – the sort that destroy and alter a true sense of self.

Whenever Ella's insecurities erupt inside herself – feelings of self-doubt and for others, the 16th century Jack Be Nimble wanders through the crowds of Memory Lane like Black Jack, an English pirate escaping not only authorities, but also responsibilities. If Ella finds herself nearly to tears, the winds that sometimes blow down Memory Lane accompany the voices of children singing: *"Rain Rain go Away."*

This song begins as a cumulonimbus cloud. It depicts the face of England's Tudor monarch Elizabeth I (1533-1603) forming in the sky, as men in Spanish uniform of this time period fall like dolls. Most of the imprints – or sorts of ghosts, who congregate in Memory Lane are unaware Ella is present in thought. She listens and watches their interviews, conversations and actions of the past, as if they had been recorded on video.

On Memory Lane, Ella sees one such housekeeper. To keep things in order, I will refer to her as Housekeeper #1.

"I've been cleaning houses for twenty-five years," she says.

This housekeeper routinely skips rooms she claims later to have cleaned. Then, she picks up her paycheck – one she deludes herself and others into believing she earns.

"Trustworthy?" Housekeeper #2 says.

"Why you won't find another cleaning woman as dependable myself."

This one's cleaning includes performing disappearing acts with valuables that are not her own. And what about Housekeeper #3? She professes, while wearing a hairnet and looking overtop thick, plastic glasses and flashing a gold-tooth smile in a manner of a talking mule:

"I'm a professional. Time is money. You owe me for my time whether or not I finish cleaning . . . . and by the way, how do you like that new scent I added to your upholstery?"

And Housekeeper #4? One day as Ella washes vegetables in the kitchen sink, this one approaches saying:

"Oh, mam, I could not find a bucket. I dipped my mop into that sink."

Ella cringes and more so when the presence of Housekeeper #5 interrupts. This one enjoys secretly granting herself bonuses and conducts regular treasure hunts. When her secret is discovered – as if she thought it would never be, she disappears much like a ghost who sees the light.

And Housekeeper #6? Her voice is quite loud:

"My specialty is cleaning picture frames!"

One day ten years ago Housekeeper #6 waltzes in. She carries a feather duster. The housekeeper's young daughter is unexpectantly with her. They are there to assist with a birthday party for Ella's eldest son. In the midst of preparations, Housekeeper #6 and her daughter polish off a gallon of juice for party attendees. The housekeeper's daughter slaps Ella's baby Aaron over a doll as Ella enters.

"I saw what you did," she responds.

"By the way, that's not your doll. It's mine."

Ella grunts her reaction through a plastered smile, glances the kitchen – specifically at Housekeeper #6 drinking down more party supplies. Ella is too distracted to mind.

Her focus is on the antics of the housekeeper's little girl. Ella gathers her baby son, a toy doll and exits. The housekeeper's daughter is smug; without remorse.

There are housekeepers who arrive late. There are those who make up excuses to leave early without finishing. They come up with all sorts of excuses as to why they must vamoose.

"I have to see my proctologist," one says.

"My taxidermist. My optometrist. My psychiatrist. My exterminator. My mechanic. My orthodontist. My plumber. My dentist."

Some push dirt with much hustle-bustle. No elbow grease. A few eat breakfast, lunch and dinner at the refrigerator, and charge for washing dishes they dirty.

"Mam? What is it you need?" one asks.

"I couldn't hear. I am chewing. Okay. (CRUNCH. CRUNCH. SMACK. POP.) *Okay, now, you can talk."*

There are the ones who pride themselves on many things. One says,

"I pride myself on being punctual, mam,"

only to find they are always punctually late or punctually absent, punctually snacking or punctually napping in the master bedroom.

On Memory Lane, Ella notices a street sign called: *"Thirteen years ago."* Ella walks up this side street and into her home of that time.

Trudare is there. She's also known as Housekeeper #7.

"Uh . . . . oh, I didn't hear you come in," she says.

Trudare scratches her head with one hand and catches the remote control with the other as she stands suddenly.

"Just taking a little napper . . . . nothing too long," she says.

"You know, this job cuts right into my soap's hour."

Trudare, who stammers, struggles with a reply.

"Housework is a tiring occupation," she says.

"There is nothing like a little time with the soaps to make one feel refreshed and ready to start back to work."

Trudare mumbles as she walks off into Cleaning Nowhere Land. Ella exits her home on Memory Lane. She notices another sign on a side street called: *"Fourteen years ago."* She walks up this street, enters her home then and finds Housekeeper #8 in the livingroom. Housekeeper #8 is the 15-year-old bride of a 38-year-old man.

"Do you attend school?" Ella asks.

Housekeeper #8, who wears dirty jeans and a tee shirt over a buxom chest, looks through a mane of stringy, oily blond hair.

"I quit," she replies.

"I needed work. I wanted out. My father was mean, mam. He shot our puppies after our momma dog gave birth. He always threatened to shoot something or someone . . . always yelling and carrying on."

Housekeeper #8, without embarrassment, possesses an attitude like a four-year-old loudly announcing bathroom business in the middle of a church service.

"Don't get me wrong," she says.

"My father put a roof over my head, food on the table. But he was always paranoid. He drank. He thought someone was trying to do him in. All along, he was this someone."

Ella glances at the scrawl across the wrinkled paper presented and clears her throat.

"Remind me again," she says.

"What's your name? I don't see it on this paper," Ella continues.

"BILLIE-BARBARA-JEAN . . . . I was named after my aunt and uncle," she answers.

Housekeeper #8 speaks with a sense of pride and importance. Her attitude clashes with the Hades she describes.

To survive in the midst of emotional instability and sore-infested demons, finding anything to be proud of is a rope that keeps the able body from sliding completely into the dust of a mountain.

Ella walks out the door of this home and passes the sign *"Fourteen years Ago."* She continues on until she runs face-to-face into William Miller holding a poster before him. It reads: *"Go back!"* As quickly as this happens, Ella feels a cat brushing against her ankles. She walks back. Ella again finds herself sitting in her livingroom of 14 years ago. A cat circles and flirts about her legs there as well too.

Ella's mind ponders how to politely escort Housekeeper #8 out. But as you might have expected, she is not allowed to do this on Memory Lane. That would be like playing God, and none of us – have such power. Housekeeper #8 says:

"Mam, I really do need a job. I promise I will work real hard if you hire me," Billie-Barbara-Jean says.

Ella grows anxious about not hurting the prospect's feelings, gazes about the ceiling and floor and breathes out a long span of air.

"Okay," she says.

"Billie-Bar bah-Jean Jo Billie-bob-john-boy or whatever your name is . . . . Well, let me allow you to work along side another housekeeper. Her plans of quitting are underway. She's here every other weekend and on college breaks. Let's see how things work out."

Housekeeper #8 makes a sigh of appreciation, smiles wide and shakes Ella's hand.

"Thank ya. I 'preciate 'dat," she says.

"Well, I reckon I'd better be get' tin outside. My husband will be pick' in me up soon. He won't walk to the door. We have errands to run."

Ella detests Billie-Barbara-Jean's personal life. She views Billie-Barbara-Jean's husband as most do a criminal. Still, sorrow envelops her over Billie-Barbara-Jean's situation. Billie-Barbara-Jean needs employment at an immature age. She is, in all certainty, an under-aged bride of a man who is clearly – clear to those of modern and normal brains, not a man of good, moral or descent character.

"It might work out having her work for us," Ella thinks.

Ella exits her home. Why should it be a surprise that directly next door to this home on *"Fourteen Years Ago"* is another side street called: *"Several days later."* Ella walks up this street and into the abode. There, she sees Housekeeper #8.

"Howdy doo, mam," she says.

"You know, there's nothin' better to clean windows with than bleach and ammonia."

Billie-Barbara-Jean speaks as she dries a glass door with paper towels. Ella runs out this home, and in such immediate frenzy, she stumbles upon a road called: *"Three Years Ago."* William Miller and his Wee Willie Winkie stand outside this home holding a sign:

"Go on, get on with it!"

Such ordeals take Ella through strings of prospects – including one who speaks English only when it suits her. Ella walks into her home then. There before her is Housekeeper #9. This prospect, reaching out to shake Ella's hand, rolls hisses at their first meeting.

"I'm CAT-AH-TEEN-NAH," housekeeper #9 says.

"I from May-eee-co. I clean for you. When start?"

Ella spies the prospect carefully.

"It's a strange thing you should appear on my doorstep," she says.

"I asked the agency not to give out my address."

Housekeeper #9 smiles nervous anticipation, avoids commenting on Ella's observation, and exaggeratedly inspects the walls.

"I clean for you, Yes? I mother too. I understand. I love to clean bathroom. This house? Lots of bathroom? You need good housekeeper? I good housekeeper. My mother eh . . . . housekeeper and earn lots of money."

Ella grins nervous politeness. Her demeanor is cautious as she nods with affirmation Catalina's enthusiasm for cleaning bathrooms.

No sooner does Ella raise her hand to adjust a piece of stray hair when she finds herself standing before a street called: *"Weeks later."* Ella sluggishly walks into the abode before her. Her husband, dressed in winter attire and standing just inside, says:

"If she is going to work this diligently, give her a raise. Make sure you pay her very well before someone steals her."

Of course, there is no mistake about the identity of the person he refers to. Ella walks upstairs. There she finds Catatina helping to fill boxes with clothing and other items from a nearby closet. Later, Ella assists Catatina with loading a chair into Catatina's car trunk.

Ella, learning of Catatina's need of household items at her own abode, is happy to help her. Ella assesses what she can afford to give away – things she and her family rarely-to-never use anymore, or had several of. It seems with each day Ella finds more to spare. Catatina is as pleased as Ella. One day Catatina asks to have certain items Ella does not wish to give away.

"You no want?" Catatina presumptively asks of a microwave oven.

"You no want! I take?"

"Oh, we still use that," Ella regretfully responds.

"You have two," Catatina insists.

"Give me one?"

With each episode of refusal of tug and pull, Catatina's cleaning takes new forms of lift, slam, dent and chip. Ella finds electrical plates smashed, cracked, torn off walls. Catatina's response is quick without a trace of remorse.

"Not work?" Catatina asks.

"Broke? My husband he know how to fix that. He fix that too? You hire my husband? He good worker."

The clacking doorknocker reveals another prospect as Ella's cat – Mister Citrouilles, hops to the doorstep. It stands idly licking its paws. Citrouilles is a medium ball of orange fluff and large orange eyes. Because most people are not privy to the thoughts of cats, I will share them.

"What do you say about this one here?" asks the cat.

"Forget me. Just note the owwww!"

Citrouilles vomits a hairball.

Exhausted, Ella walks to the door and leaves. She's been ready to leave Memory Lane for the past hour. She walks down Memory Lane and sees a sign called: *"Four years ago."* Inside her home then, Housekeeper #10 steps toward Ella. With her hand extended in an apprehensive manner, she says,

"I'm Lux Bux."

Ella, extending her hand in cautious politeness and disbelief, replies:

"Really? Is that your given name? Your real name?"

Housekeeper #10 answers,

"Yes, my mother named me for her aunt."

Ella asks,

"That would be your great aunt?"

Housekeeper #10 Lux Bux says:

"Yeah. Yes. That's right. Her name is Lux. Then, wouldn't you know? I married a Bux. Now, I'm Lux Bux."

Ella presses her lips inward and pauses to gather her composure.

"What experience do you have cleaning houses?" she asks.

Looking about the floor and then the ceiling for what seems a lengthy time to search one's brain for an answer, Lux replies:

"Well . . . . well. Hmm. I clean for my aunt. I live with my aunt, and I clean for her . . . I clerked a bit. Uh. Hm."

Ella, blotting her nose with a tissue, waits for further comments.

"Oh, I see," Ella responds when it is clear Lux has nothing more to add.

"I can learn if you will show me how you want things done," Lux says.

"I need this job."

"Okay," Ella replies.

"Okay," Ella repeats caving in with a sigh of lost faith. An apprehensive, half-attempt grin forms on Ella's face. Could it be negativity waits to stomp her back again?

"Maybe you can help me out?" Ella affirms.

Ella opens the front door to leave and spies William Miller. She might not have recognized him, but he toted a copy of his Scottish nursery rhyme *"Wee Willie Winkie"* under his arm and dressed as the character he depicted in the 1841. He holds a poster board containing the words: *"Weeks later."* Ella closes the door, walks into the livingroom, where she finds Lux more interested in eating, sitting and borrowing items she never returns. Ella shows Lux how to clean. Lux puts her feet up and takes another bite of banana.

"You know," Lux says, before swallowing,

"You clean better than I do."

Ella nods worried acknowledgement. Lux's feet are a field of bumps, bunions and fungus. At every opportunity, Lux places her feet high in flip-flops, eats meals and makes messes.

"I didn't get much sleep," says Lux when haphazardly walked in upon.

"I can see you get a lot done without me. I woke today with a terrible appetite. No time to eat. Like I always say, be on time, no matter what. What do you have to eat around here?"

Lux stands, walks to the kitchen and opens the refrigerator door. Ella follows, prepares a sandwich, pours a glass of water and says,

"While you are eating, you are not on the clock."

One day Lux disappears. She seems to dissolve to rain. Her telephone is disconnected. She vanishes without explanation or forwarding address. She leaves along with a couple of VHS tapes. One of the tapes is titled: *"Imposters,"* and the other: *"A Fish Called Wanda."* For Ella, Lux reveals herself to be an imposter, an actor or liar, a thief like Wanda.

Finally, Ella walks out the front door of her home in Memory Lane, makes her way back to her current abode, and stretches across her bed. Maybe a dream or two will allow her Soul and Spirit opportunity to wash negativity down the drain.

Chapter 10

Deciphering Webs

A S YOU MIGHT BE able to relate, memories can be just as disturbing as dreams. When Ella stretches across her bed, travels transport her into another season, where wind and rain blow in torrents. Water accumulates to fierce flooding. Walls melt like hardened sugars against the splash of lime punch. Trees bend to snapping. Holes form in walls like miniature doorways for birds. The darkened earth is beneath murky, green liquid. Waters rise until her home resembles a submerged houseboat.

At 9 a.m. the following morning, Ella sits at her desk. As she writes, she feels as if her home is a glass house. It fills with water. Furnishings float well above the average height of a man. It empties like a fish tank, as if it contains a drain. Ella writes:

"I feel panic. I leap. I run
a race with rising water.
There is a green house. There,
my eldest sons appear as ages
seventeen and twenty. They play
a board game with their father
amongst the plants. Echoes of
my voice call: 'Run! Save your
lives!'"

In such a dream, the ceiling of the greenhouse crashes inward as her sons run to the stairwell to climb to safety. Broken glass and splashing waters gush like on an obstacle course of slides and ramps.

Ella writes:

*"Then, they appear as they are
now at ages thirteen and ten.
They are safe in my arms within
the walls of eroding sugar. With
God, I guard them. I am going to
sleep to decipher webs of this
dream; perhaps a reflection of
inner chaos."*

Chapter II

Miss V. Rae & the Storm

ELLA'S SEARCH FOR A housekeeper continues through the seasons. Years prior to Ella's recent search brought three children – two in March and one in September, with the expected and unexpected messes life dips up.

One autumn day around 5 p.m., Ella receives company in her livingroom. Ella sits with a friend – Miss V. Rae. She confides experiences of hiring and firing housekeepers. Ella confides her frustrations to Miss V. Rae who nods occasionally and throws in:

"Yes, I understand."

As Ella speaks – the wind's speed coincidently increases, blowing a shutter off the house into the crevices of boxwood. They lodge like pirates' planks bending against the windy undertow of invisible wings.

The mailbox sways with its red flag rattling into a blur. Still, Ella talks unaware, as Miss V. Rae nervously glances the windows.

The wind blows with explosive passion. It tears a gutter off a neighboring house. It knocks a few shingles amongst debris flying like a witch on a broom in the neighboring winds of a tornado. The wind's fury is like a giant sigh of a tuberculin-plague infested cough carrying and debriding Ella's burdens to far off lands.

DISHONEST HOUSEKEEPERS | 63

Spirit and Soul, who stand side by side, look out a window as Ella and Miss V. Rae converse. Spirit, dressed in a yellow raincoat and rain hat, gazes trees bending in the wind. Soul, dressed in a long nightshirt and nightcap, holds a closed umbrella.

"When Mother or Father Nature get involved. Well, just look at their paths!" Spirit says.

Soul yawns.

"Nice weather," he says.

"Very nice."

The swaying trees, creak, crack, bump and thump. A face forms in the clouds unknown to Ella and Miss V. Rae. As the wind blows, this shadowy image – faintly noticeable, runs itself like a ghost dancing across the top of a hedge. It glides across the sky gazing through bare and dressed branches. It leaves Ella's town. It travels through several snows of winter and in places where weather conditions don't change much from one season to the next.

The shadowy image travels through pollen storms of April and heat-lightening storms of summer and the crispy-sleeted winds of October and November. It travels through mountains and over streams and oceans as waves wildly crash foreign shores.

Ella seems hardly concerned about the rising storm outside. She continues talking, as the weather's fury seems to mimic frustration. Even after Ella tells her friend good-bye and turns in for the night, the storm grows.

The storm spreads like multiple twisters traveling the world. It unleashes itself into ocean waves to the other side of the Atlantic. It is as if Ella's words ride waves that smash ports of foreign lands. Some call this coincidence, bad karma or mojoe. It is, nevertheless, a calling to put right – to change negativity that stirs like moldy sweet and sour soup in a hot caldron.

Chapter 12

The Advertisement

IT IS A BEAUTIFUL fall day. On a train, if you are a passenger, you can see two hands holding a newspaper. But who might this be? Well, it is none other than Lux Bux. So, we see she really does know how to read! A careless remark, I know. But if you have sympathy for Ella, and I assume you do, you understand.

There dotted about this train car are various passengers from all walks of life. There are mothers, fathers, children, grandparents, students, a couple of teachers, a nurse, doctor, dentist, businessman, banker, farmer, janitor, inventor, engineer, mathematician, chemist, architect, plumber, beautician, private investigator, electrician, journalist, editor, genealogist, car salesman, coalmine and aluminum workers, a computer analyst and several others.

If you can pretend for a moment you are either amongst this group or possibly a ghost or some form of other innocent bystander, look over the top of Lux's newspaper. It says:

DOMESTIC HELP NEEDED
AT IRISH ESTATE. ROOM &
BOARD INCLUDED WITH
SALARY. EXPERIENCE
REQUIRED. SEND INQUIRIES
IN CARE OF THIS NEWSPAPER.

As you might deduce, the fate of dishonest housekeepers, whether they pass through Ella's world or not, is beyond another door – far beyond the train's exit. By the way, did you hear the conductor's call? He yelled:

"Next stop! Chapter Thirteen!"

See you there. I need to powder my nose and throw a couple of salt pinches across my shoulder.

Chapter 13

Across Land & Ocean

HAVE YOU EVER TRAVELED to Haworth, England? If so, in winter? If not, as I must assume you either have or have not, and knowing that is totally within your own experiences – BUT if you have not, my plan includes describing it.

In Haworth, there is a village cemetery, just down from Brontë house. In winter, it seems to be a rather dark, blue-gray place. Within its buildings, are happy people, though, who radiate the sunshine they need to carry them through winter or any gray day England's weather dishes out.

The place Lux will travel to is *not* to Haworth, but to a place very similar. It is a place that reminds me a lot of Haworth, but a place you will never find on a map. The path dishonest housekeepers end up on resembles what one might find in Brontë's *"Wuthering Heights,"* or on the breath of tiny winds in Haworth, where Charlotte, Anne and Emily worked their novels out in the eighteen forties.

The ivy around this estate door is thick. This estate is in Ireland, which we know is a far cry from Haworth. Ireland seems to always be rich in vibrant greens even in the dead of winter. It's a place where rains fall daily. Where potato-leek-dishwater soup and misty-cold are as predictable as waves tilting cargo across the Irish Sea. This estate is, I emphasize, unknown to Irish citizens – except those who travel here one way or another.

It seems that Billie-Barbara-Jean, who goes to work at a hospital after leaving her employment in Ella's abode, finds her way to this estate. She arrives after answering the same ad Lux reads. Catatina, as well, finds her way as she improves her English. She wins a raffle ticket that pays for the voyage.

I must back up one stop and clarify to catch you up, it seems. Lux, while working for another employer discovers a wad of cash tucked away in a vase. Her sticky fingers locate extra cash. As a result, she is offered a special deal she cannot resist: One of her employers allows a pardon if she promises never to return. With no place to go, she discovers an advertisement. It, of course, leads her across the ocean.

Chapter 14

The Secret Irish Estate

IF YOU WILL, IMAGINE standing in front of the door of the Irish estate – the one you will not find on a map – the one you will never find unless you are or come to be a dishonest housekeeper. Of course, I hope you never require a housekeeper, or become one unless you desire to be an honest one and if you are particularly talented with such tasks.

So, one by one, dishonest housekeepers and others with questionable housekeeping practices walk a pathway to a front door. It is as if they are compelled to travel here by something they can't explain, other than the need for employment.

The pathway through brilliant green landscapes is in fact painted along side nature's cruel thorns. There are rows of bloomless roses. Upon entering, each prospect glances the walls. The walls are papered in daffodils ceiling-to-foot. Vases in the entrance hall display daffodils and other yellow flowers not grown on the estate; some are black. Yellow is a color of friendship for some, remorse for others. Black is, well, rather dark.

In the entrance or foyé is a small replica of Auguste Rodin's *"THE THINKER"* adorning a marble table. The feet on this statue, however, have two very noticeable – obnoxiously so, bunions not sculpted on the larger original.

Do not believe for a second this replica sculpture sits idly by for the beauty of it. Its presence emphasizes this estate is a special place – a locality, where thinking caps materialize no matter how much rebellion one demonstrates.

In a corner of the foyé is a tall grandfather clock. If anyone stares too intently at the clock, his or her face transforms into the face of the clock. As they notice, however, it transforms itself back to its original state, prompting onlookers to rub their eyes and re-focus.

Now, if you recall, I asked you to imagine you stand in front of this estate door. The door is opening so maybe you need not imagine anymore – just observe. In this story, we are the observers. I have no intention of ever being a dishonest housekeeper, and neither should you! We all, I admit, male or female, child or adult, whether by true profession or not, unless we are a king or queen or a spoiled prince, must learn to clean up after ourselves. In this sense, we are all housekeepers of some degree. Well, let's get on with it. (That's an expression I hear in my head from my own childhood. My mother used to say this when she wanted me to continue.)

A nameless female person opens the door – a well-oiled and refined door it is too!

"Welcome," the woman says.

"Are you friend, neighbor, traveler or foe?"

Let's step inside along with this visitor. This woman answering the door, or those ringing the doorbell can't acknowledge us. They are not capable of seeing us, and in this sense, we are like ghosts.

If you have not noticed yet, the nameless person never identifies herself. She looks remarkably similar to Ella. Of course, she is not. Ella rests quietly on the other side of the earth. Again, believe me, it's not her! Know, however, Ella, although sleeping better these days, is growing quite content. But I sense you can't possibly be content. You are wondering where am I taking you on this journey?

Rest assured, there are no wild geese here. Those are reserved for *"Memory Lane."* I strongly advise, however, you pay attention to colors, symbols and foreshadowing tools because this story is chalked full. Also, I advise you read the *"For Your Information"* pages at the end of this book!

Chapter 15

Eve of Resolution

DAY LIGHT POURS INTO the livingroom windows. The kitchen is another scene altogether. The blinds are drawn in there to camouflage dishes piled about the sink. Ella sits in front of a round coffee table and swirls her index finger through pollen dust.

Exhausted from mommy-duties, Ella resolves dishes, laundry and dust can pile a mile before she will hire help again. Some resolutions are temporary. When she can list in pollen dust names of those hired prior, she might reconsider. After all, she's not Joan Cleaver or Donna Reed or Superwoman. She's just Ella – a writer who strives every day of her life to create, write, edit, research – but foremost, to love her family with all respect they are entitled to.

Okay, let's get on with it.

Chapter 16

Mister Hedgecroft

IT'S 4 P.M. ON THE clock in the foyé of this secret Irish estate. You might feel a bit medieval walking through its giant entrance. If you are allowed to sit, you might suddenly feel a bit Victorian – but you will definitely not feel the modern comforts of heat. The walls in this place seem to hold cold like an icebox. If you must, put on an extra pair of socks.

The woman who answers the door says little-to-anything. She points arrivals towards the estate's overseer. Each newly arrived prospect speaks of best skills, qualities and interests. They behave as if they are not sure they have the job. I assure you they do. They are very *qualified* to have ended up here. We, on the other hand, are not – except for the small spiritual token of appreciation granted to me in relaying this story.

If you will, look to the middle of this entrance. That's right. There is Mr. Edwin Hedgecroft. He is indeed a strong, medium-sized sight for sore eyes. (To me, he is an angel in disguise.) He walks with purpose and looks directly into the eyes of each housekeeper – as if he has waited uncomplainingly.

"I'm head butler and overseer here," he addresses the housekeepers.

"If you need anything, direct concerns to me day or night. Before we get you all settled and onto your work here, we require a brief review of expected tasks."

Hedgecroft, dressed in modern black attire for a domestic, glides the palm of his hand across the wet-gloss of his dark gothic do. It is spliced with long white strands along a high forehead.

Hedgecroft retrieves a white handkerchief from an interior chest pocket, wipes his hands, then tucks it back into place. He stretches, rests his arms behind his back, glances his feet momentarily, walks across the room and opens a closet. He retrieves a stiff broom and walks to face each newcomer with a little smile of acknowledgment.

Directing himself to the prospects that form a line in the foyé, Hedgecroft clears his throat.

"What sorts of brooms have you been privy to use?" he asks.

He lays out an array of broom sorts – flat ones, soft bristles, straw ones, angular, spider web brushes, et cetera.

Hedgecroft regards this job of cleaning as seriously as one who takes exams in chemistry, mathematics or literature, or as one who teaches, or one who diagnoses, or one who counsels, or one who builds, or invents.

He holds up a mop, then, an assortment of scrub brushes and cleaning solutions.

*"I'm sure all of you are aware, one **never** mixes bleach or chlorine with ammonia or products containing ammonia,"* he says.

"To do so, creates a deadly gas."

He speaks as he looks coincidentally into the direction of Billie Barbara-Jean. Then, Hedgecroft moves his focus into Lux's direction.

"We all know, of course, never to eat and clean at the same time," he says.

"This is unsanitary – not only for you – but for our employer."

Without batting an eye – Hedgecroft speaks the next coincidence:

"Bananas and other such foods are to be eaten only during meals and breaks."

Hedgecroft – walking in a horizontal line in front of the housekeepers, straightens and stretches his fingers connecting one hand to the other, pauses briefly, glances the clock, then trails his eyes back to the prospects.

He grasps the edges of his vest, pulls downward to flatten the front panels, inhales deeply, and then exhales slowly. As he exhales, the wind kicks up slightly. It rattles a window. Hedgecroft walks to the window, secures the lock, and returns to the housekeepers. All continue to stand comfortably in a row.

"Great care should be taken not to damage properties," Hedgecroft says with a most peculiar and pensive expression.

"Don't bang brooms, mops and vacuums into the feet and sides of furnishings or into baseboards or walls. This chips and dents. Special care should be made. Do not clank dishes or handle properties in depreciative manners. Do not flush dirty mop water down toilets or sinks. Mail, check books, pocket books and personal drawers are off limits. Keep these things in mind."

As Hedgecroft speaks, the clock lapses and now reads: *"5 p.m."* His list continues on and on, until he runs out of steam. Within the hour, he yawns. Hedgecroft walks softly across the floor. His demeanor is what some might interpret as Native American. He is a soft and gentle personae. His core, however, is strong, yielding to those with a willingness to learn.

Hedgecroft's noble and gracious demeanor puts others of honorable character at ease. For those of ill, crafty or ignorant intentions, Hedgecroft is perceived as an easy obstacle. Unknown to the prospects, his courage is that of a lion – a team of angels. Hedgecroft's peculiarity and awkwardness is overshadowed by his purpose to provide influence. He is, nevertheless, secretly repulsed by what he senses.

The hands of the clock now rest at 7 p.m. and are company to several yawns.

"Thank you," Hedgecroft says.

"I leave you to discover your new home and obligations. With one more word to the wise, a sort of advisement, if you will, clock-watching is frowned upon. Every employee is paid well here, so there is simply no need for it."

Excuse me for yawning. Clouds and rain have such an effect on me. I advise, however, you keep yawns to yourself. If we offend Mr. Hedgecroft, we might find ourselves permanent residents of this estate. Of course, he has no idea we are here. Most likely, he is unable to hear or to see us.

Billie-Barbara-Jean takes such an assignment with great pride as she picks up her bags. She speaks in a manner, which suggests she is a follower of a backwoods Baptist church setting sail on a new adventure. Her manner is that of a spiritually lost person seeking religion.

"Mister Hedgecroft, show me the way," she says.

Ella's former prospects each outwardly show eagerness to learn and work. They are; however, flawed. They are ignorant of common sense, or devoid of remorse for wrongdoing. They are craftsmen at hiding this during interviews and employment.

Days unfold into months and years. The pathway to this estate brings those who possessed employment from Ella, as well as other dishonest housekeepers employed by others.

It rains frequently in Ireland. What more can I say about this? You accompany me on this journey in black and white, so I must emphasize things such as weather. I must also emphasize colors and that you carry in your backpack an umbrella, galoshes and earmuffs. Can you see it now? The colors! The greens are like no other in the world, but the roses remain budless at this estate.

Chapter 17

To Dream is to Fly

IT IS NECESSARY NOW that you enter one of Ella's dreams. It is her personal venture to record them. So on this note, be advised we are in a public park, mind your shoelaces and that fly – the one on your shoulder. The weather is sunny with partially cloudy skies, gusty winds. The park contains benches. Tree branches sway in a breeze. I love to gaze in open skies, but not this one.

Here rains will soon develop and mix with winds, but not before this next transition. Ella walks here with her children. Red cars without wheels glide like planes without wings.

There are four such contraptions. One glides over the tops of trees. This happens just as Ella notices Chris walks across a grassy slope. He sits, stretches against the grass, yawns and is oblivious to the flying cars. (If we yell, "*Wake up!*" he won't hear us.)

Ella, noticing the cars aim like kamikaze pilots, pulls Aaron under a park bench. The cars leak fluid. One sprays a green liquid. It turns red and drips like blood. Ella wakes and begins recording this dream experience.

"It gets on my skin. It is
cold at first. Then, I fear
it will burn us. I hold my

son's face close. I wake.
He is asleep. The cars
disappear. We are safe."

Ella continues to write. Her mind is enveloped in the scenery of a park after a storm. She holds her journal, as the park fades from her thoughts.

Chapter 18

The Fate of Lux Bux

IT IS A WINTER day at the Irish estate. The rooms of the prospects here coincidently contain duplicate items they once stole or borrowed, not only from Ella – but from others. The most insensitive thing amongst this lot is none immediately takes notice. They tuck items into apron pockets or secretively into cleaning caddies.

Housekeepers hide loots in varying places. When they return to duties, they find the same items picked up the day before are returned to original places. Their recognition is much to their improvement. They are unable to look directly into Hedgecroft's eyes. He seemingly suspects nothing. With paranoia, the housekeepers believe otherwise.

These housekeepers squirm like nervous misfits in anticipation of having to look into the eyes of the unidentified woman. She passes through corridors and halls like a ghost saying *little-to-nothing*, but smiling. If she says anything at all, it is:

"I hope you are enjoying your stay."

Hired prospects retire each evening. On their nightstands is a copy of this book – not in its entirety, but enough of this story as can be allowed. Its cover contains the title at the blank side space right of a housekeeper's face.

The actual face on each cover reveals that of the housekeeper whose room it is in. Her features include what one might imagine Paul-Revere's hair-do to have been; ears like Icabod Crane sporting a ponytail with a black-velvet ribbon at its tip. Most note a book there – but never venture to open it. Had they ventured to take a little peek, they might have imagined what awaited them – their futures here.

In the estate's corridor one day, Lux Bux passes a hall mirror. As Lux cleans, she stops to look at her reflection. She notices her skin flaking and unusually dry. She is puzzled. Her concern is to the point she seeks direction.

"Mister Hedgecroft?" she asks.

"Is there a doctor about this property or one nearby?"

As Hedgecroft makes his way through the corridors inspecting the quality of work being done, he brushes a drape with his hand as if to knock out dust. He wipes a windowsill, and then turns his hand to inspect for possible dust.

"Why, yes," he replies.

"There are several. I imagine housekeepers require a podiatrist from time to time."

Lux glances at her feet, and then gazes at Hedgecroft.

"Possibly later, sir," she says.

"At present, I'm in need of a dermatologist; a very good one if you know what I mean?"

"Yes," Hedgecroft replies.

Hedgecroft wishes not to interfere as he jots a list on paper, and then hands it to her.

"I understand. Here's a list of those in the area. You can begin making calls during your break."

As night falls, Lux makes her way across town. She passes through a graveyard and carries the list of physicians tightly in her fist. Without the slightest anticipation, she stumbles over rocks and falls flat on her stomach. With her chin an inch from the ground, she reads the epitaph of a stone before her:

"Here our dear maid will rest if she ever does."

Lux reads nervously in dim light, then struggles to stand. A passerby in a long, dark gray suit coat and black brimmed hat stretches out a gloved hand.

"Are you lost?" he asks.

"Allow me. Please, to help you."

Lux reaches. The stranger pulls her to stand. His face disappears in a blurry haze of a dark hat and cloudy surroundings. Lux leans forward to see more. She nods a polite, nervous acknowledgement, and then walks away. Lux finds her way to a local physician who recommends over-the-counter remedies, using rubber gloves and soaking in oatmeal baths.

As everyone knows, winter days can be harsh on skin. Lux follows her doctor's advice and soaks in water mixed with oatmeal powder.

As cloudy water drains from the tub, Lux searches through toiletries. She seems in great haste to find something she lost. Stopping only to adjust her frumpy robe and the towel wrapped about her head, Lux rummages through boxes and old suitcases.

Days later, Lux's condition grows worse. Nothing helps. Her eyes dim, and her hair turns to scales. Lux fumbles and scrabbles through cosmetics and hair products. What is she doing? It appears she wonders whether she has developed an allergic reaction? Looking at her a little closer, I see her pupils forming a different contour like a possum staring into headlights. Could it be she is paranoid or hysterical?

She gazes into the mirror and can no longer endure what she sees. Her image deteriorates, and she finds herself seeking slumber. I am sure you have known of people who glance into mirrors and see things their peers do not see. Could this be part of her problem?

Chapter 19

Faugh-a-Ballagh!

ONE DAY, AFTER WAITING an hour, Catatina, at the insistence of Hedgecroft, goes to look for Lux. She had not shown for breakfast or work. On Lux's bed appears a snake at least eleven and a half feet long. Catatina runs down the corridor. She searches for others to point out her discovery to and later returns to Lux's bedroom with Hedgecroft.

"Are my eyes deceiving me?" he asks.

"This can't be! There are no snakes in all of Ireland!" Hedgecroft exclaims.

"No snakes here?" Catatina asks.

"Here's one – you see? With your eyes, your very own? Yes?"

Hedgecroft pauses as he wraps his tongue over his upper front teeth.

"Y . . . . Yes, but what sense can we make of this?" he asks.

"This snake frightened Lux away; this is for certain," Catatina responds.

Hedgecroft paces about the hall just outside Lux's room, bites his lower lip, blinks his eyes in an anxious fashion, and stares as if gathering his thoughts before speaking.

"Ireland's patron Saint Patrick ran all the snakes out a very long time ago, says Hedgecroft, *"but of course, if you don't believe in such spells or abilities, biologists and geologists say Ireland was isolated in the last Ice Age by glaciation. This killed off snakes that never found their way back across the Irish Sea to the mainland of the British Isles. I guess, I suppose there is a first for everything."*

Hedgecroft shrugs his shoulders, tilts his head as if to ponder another thought, walks to the doorway of Lux's room and draws a deep breath.

He rolls his sleeves, stands decisively next to the bed, nervously turns around, and then paces the room to draw courage in his hesitation. He breathes in a deep breath, then shouts:

"Faugh-a-Ballagh! Faugh-a-Ballagh!"

[Pronounced: Fah-lah-ba-lah]

Even though Catatina does not understand what this means, she is inspired by it to *"get out of the way!"*

Hedgecroft grabs the snake by its tail. He throws it hard out an opened window into the yard below. There, it slithers about the thorns. Faintly in the distance, the words are heard: *"FAUGH-A-BALLAGH!"* repeating as if from a bird's throat parroting the sound like echoes of crows in a cornfield. In the sky, a swarm of black shadows stretch like wings of a pterodactyl shadowing the green turf. They are coming in for a landing.

A closer look reveals black crows and buzzards brave enough to venture around what they perceive as a long, thick worm. They gather it into their beaks, fly across the endless dark-blue sky to their nests in higher lands far away.

Hedgecroft wipes his hands with a handkerchief before turning his attentions to Lux's disappearance. It appears she vanishes with no forwarding address, a disconnected cell phone and no explanation. He walks a corridor, stops and then picks up his employer's suit coat and hat from a nearby bench.

Chapter 20

Fates of Jesse, Catatina & Billie-Barbara-Jean

ON A WINTER'S DAY – around eight o'clock in the morning, housekeepers of the Irish estate go about their days cleaning, borrowing, looting, and often pretending to clean. Jesse, finds herself eating as she usually does – only this day such eating prompts an unusual circumstance. She finds she is unable to exit her room. Her body does not fit through the door!

Hedgecroft, while making his rounds finds Jesse. Shocked and taken aback, he stumbles, stutters, stops and starts.

"We! Ah, we," he says.

"We can't very well widen the door – this door, anymore than what it was originally."

Hedgecroft walks down the corridor as if in deep thought to solve Jesse's dilemma. Jesse's bedroom at the Irish estate is like most all of the bedrooms at this estate. Maid quarters are furnished nicely in dark poster beds. The walls have a medieval theme in both architecture and decoration.

This housekeeper resolves to sit in her room. She wobbles to her bed. It collapses into dust when she sits. Jesse attempts to pull herself up as she notices a book glaring straight at her as if it turns its cover to her attention.

The eyes of the housekeeper on the book cover blink. Jesse does not at first notice. The book pulls itself upright on the nightstand. Its spine is now perpendicular to the ceiling. Its cover faces Jesse. As Jesse glances the opposite direction, the book taps itself against the nightstand. Jesse turns attentions to the book's title:

"FATES OF DISHONEST HOUSEKEEPERS."

Lard on the housekeeper's arms is thick and wags like a dog's tail. Unable to bend her arms to reach the book, she desires something to occupy her time. Her reach strains her face to red. So, Jesse sits and sighs. What else can she do?

Her eyes fill with tears, and her nose runs. Tears roll down her fat face. A puddle of water forms on the floor. Jesse glances into it. For a brief moment, she is nearly certain she sees a face that is not her own looking back.

Perhaps, she recalls a cousin? It appears as one thinner than her own. It bares a resemblance. Within a moment, the face changes to an unmistakable glutton – one far fatter with a pink pig's snout. It drips with mucus and other unsightly gooey things.

Hair-prickly ears occupy the edges of this unpleasant reflection. The reflection takes bites from a turkey drumstick like England's King Henry the Eighth in one hand. It slurps and burps an oversized strawberry frosty with the other. The wind trails in through a window. It dries her face and the puddle. Jesse faints. (I think I would as well!)

Jesse's slumber pulls her into another house – a house of dreams. Stairs go up. Stairs go down. Escalators and elevators go up and down. The ceiling, covered in helium balloons, faces the floor speckled with air balloons that drift and creep. Strong winds lift balloons into the air, as the room grows sunny. One of the balloons pops. Snow falls. Wind blows. Jesse climbs accumulating snow and rolls. Snow sticks to her as she grows into a giant snowball with little-fat feet and little-pudgy bulges for hands sticking out the sides.

Jesse lugs her snowball body around. She settles back on her cold, round rump. She drifts to sleep again as she rolls about like a balloon – unaware of her movements.

Some hours later, she wakes in her room in a puddle of water – a wee bit smaller and a wee bit stronger. It is around 7 p.m., and the puddle is quite cold from the winter breezes that occasionally leak through small crevices between windows, walls and floors. Jesse is still too large to fit through the door.

Jesse is not forgotten. Mr. Hedgecroft has spent the day speaking with an engineer and pondering over a possible solution of using olive oil to ease her through. He consults as well a dietician, who prescribes celery, watercress, lettuce and water for four months in case any plan the engineer comes up with fails.

IN ANOTHER ROOM OF this estate, Catatina observes her clock. A full moon with a bright purple night sky is present. For a brief moment, she catches glimpse of her own face transparently overtop a clock's face – but she dismisses this – believing she is *very* tired. She glances through her window into the sky at the moon. Briefly, her face appears transparently transposed over it. She rubs her eyes – believing she needs fresh air.

Catatina opens her window. The scene she views is not the garden outside the estate. She sees the interior of a church. A saintly and sympathetic priest, flanked by pews, stands in the aisle before her.

"Do you wish to confess something?" she asks.

Distracted, Catatina gazes at church treasures. She is in complete awe and mostly of disbelief. Her greed grows as she walks through the window that has grown into a door. She steps around the priest, ignoring him and his question. She gazes up, down, around. She steals an offering box and returns to her room.

Catatina places the box on her bed and looks at the doorway in which she found her way back. Only the original window appears. As the box melts in thin air, Catatina, enraged, slams a table against a wall – cracking the plate of an outlet cover. She stretches her arms across a dressing table in a manner of desperation.

The cracked plate rises from the wall, as it grows larger until a cave-like entrance forms. A ghostly door swings open. A violent wind holds Catatina's attention and astonishment. The wind flips her hair out of its holder – blowing it about her head and face like Medusa's mane.

A sucking gust with a determined voice of reckoning whisks her back into the church. There, she is held inside a confessional booth by unseen forces at work.

On the other side of the screen transposed overtop of the priest are the ghost-like faces of all who have employed her – looking back at her, waiting for her to speak.

Catatina is wide-eyed with a frightful stare fixated on the screen, where the priest sits.

"Well, go on child, what is it, you wish to confess?" he asks.

One green-gray face looks through the screen directly into her eyes – with eyes that resemble those of the ghost of Marley in Charles Dickens' *A Christmas Carol.*

"Go on, tell us," he encourages.

The priest leans his head against the wall, turns and leans his face towards the screen, peers directly at Catatina and straightens the crucifix draped over his robe.

"Go on child," he says.

"What are you waiting for? Christmas? It's come and gone. It's just me here with God, Jesus, the Virgin Mary and the Saints. We don't bite – even if you do. Come on now. What is it you have to say?"

The transposed figure Catatina sees widens her bulging eyes. Catatina starts and stammers because in her reckoning, she recognizes faces of those who question her. Perspiration beads about her forehead and shining dark-black hair.

"Has a jaguar got your tongue?" the priest inquires.

"Perhaps, a bear? The devil? Now, come on. Get on with it. We've actually got years, but why delay?"

Transposed overtop the priest's face, the image of a man's cat face (favoring Citrouilles') appears. It fades back to the priest's natural face.

"No hablo inglés," Catatina says.

"No English. No hablo inglés. No English."

"That's okay," the priest replies.

"We speak any language you do."

A voice retorts through the screen. Catatina resolves she is going to be there quite some time. Her issues run deep. She has much explaining to do – in Spanish or English. An apology is no doubt in order. The priest understands both.

BY NOW YOU MAY be asking yourself what has happened to Billie-Barbara-Jean? Well, you are in luck because I am about to tell you. On the highest floor of the estate – Billie-Barbara-Jean stretches. She yawns and drifts in and out of sleep. Distracted by yelping – not the sort indicative of pain – but the variety that comes from little innocent creatures calling their mothers.

With Fred Flintstone toes and Johnny Cake Ho feet, Billie-Barbara-Jean stands and paces her room. Within seconds, she is again in bed. She stretches her arms to the ceiling while sitting up. She hesitates as her attention and eyes drift to the door.

Billie-Barbara-Jean is terribly frustrated as she pushes herself out of bed. She walks to the door and grasps the knob – turning it slowly; cautiously. In front of the door on the floor is a basket of puppies. Each is happier than the first. They tumble and roll over the basket's edges.

Billie-Barbara-Jean squats next to the puppies and picks each up – cradling them against her face and chest. She glances momentarily across the room to a wall-length mirror. The mirror mysteriously grows dark. It shadows reflections it held moments prior. Billie-Barbara-Jean is curious as she stands and walks to the mirror.

The mirror begins to lighten again as she holds one puppy. In the mirror, she sees another face – it is different than her own. She looks around the edges of the mirror.

"Is this a trick or a game?" she mumbles.

Why can't she see her own reflection? The mirror again grows dark. To her right, she sees a woman. The woman is covered in pastel green-bluish feathers. The feathers grow from her skin like a bird's. The feathered woman gazes into her face. Without further delay, she hands Billie-Barbara-Jean a book.

She glances the book and again to where the feathered woman stands. She finds her gone. Shocked, Billie-Barbara-Jean rubs her eyes and glances the clock in disbelief. She places the puppies into a basket and drags it to the bed. Ella climbs onto the bed while holding a puppy against her chest with one hand and the book open with the opposite hand. She reads and drifts to sleep.

It appears I need a break from this story, as it is beginning to feel like aliens landing from outer space. Also, I have to shower and change my clothes. All those feathers gave me a bit of a rash!

What you need to know at this point is that similar fates take hold of every housekeeper who travels to this estate. Countrysides begin to reveal snakes. They hide from those who live there – except for birds whose job it is to go about collecting them. Possums and rodents that meet up with such snakes find similar fates.

One day a native Irishman – a sheep farmer, makes his way up a hilly pasture. It's a clear, bright morning. Holding a homemade staff used as a cane, he glances the distant sky and focuses on birds.

At first, he is alarmed. He fears perhaps one of his sheep is injured. A closer look reveals an inspiring sight. He rubs his crystal white-blue eyes and attempts another focus for clarification.

"What's this?" he asks himself.

"In all me days? Is it possible I require a nap this early morning?"

The birds carry flexible shadows that appear to be pieces of cloth – as he knows what he sees can't possibly be snakes! He is indeed an Irishman. As every Irish man, woman and child knows – there are no snakes in all of Ireland.

The Irish sheep farmer goes about his business. He dismisses what he has seen as something he cannot seem to get a clear picture of. He scratches his head and closes his eyes briefly before continuing.

Chapter 21

Buzzards, Possums & Weasels

SPRING HAS ARRIVED AT Ella's home on the other side of the earth. She and her sons walk into the garden. They notice roses in full bloom. To their bewildered amazement – thorns are nowhere to be found. Devil's weed is nowhere to be found either. Ella, looking at the front lawn, sees a woman walking on the path towards the garden.

"Hello," she says.

"That's a nice dog you have there. What do you call her?"

The woman walking her dog is dressed in hiking pants and a tee shirt printed with the words: *"HONESTY IS MY POLICY."*

"Eagle, replies the woman, *"I call her this because she rescued a woman from a buzzard's nest."*

Ella looks at the woman with complete astonishment.

"This woman has lost the wheels from her brand new roller skates," Ella thinks to herself.

"A buzzard's nest?" Ella questions in disbelief.

"A woman? Of all the tall tales I've heard. That one there is certainly the tallest. A grand giant, it is. Without doubt."

The woman conveys a grand story. A casual walk leads her to climb a hill in Ireland. Her dog is along for the adventure. Dust rises. High winds swirl. Tornadoes hit. At the last yards of terrain, the dog vanishes. The woman falls, as she is overwhelmed. She sleeps as the storm encircles in a hazy wreathe.

The woman walking her dog sits on a large, white rock. She continues with her story as the dog stretches, rests and occasionally eyes the cat.

"I wake to find I am inside a giant buzzard's nest," she says.

"Each buzzard has a voice. Short of one telling the other to pass ketchup and tabasco, they debate which part to dine upon.

"Giant black crows perch. They sharpen their orange beaks on rocks. They view me as a snake with a side of possum tar-tar and Mexican rodent à là king.

"My dog's barking travels closer," she explains.

"The birds fly away. I walk down. Pollen and hail fall. Wind nearly rips my jacket off. I see a woman pass. I yell, 'Stop!'

"She looks back, and I see my face straight on! My life plays in seconds. I see hurt inflicted on me and by me. Without excuses or rose-colored spectacles. I realize destiny. No matter what others dictate. What matters is who we need to be. We must focus and walk alone. Eventually, we must."

Ella looks at the woman in humored skepticism.

"Well," she says.

"Fine. Just dandy. It does not explain why you call her Eagle?"

"On that day, she rises above the storm, like Eagles flying above rain clouds," the woman continues.

"Like Eagles flying above petty things. Like eagles rising above storms. She looks down and sees sparrows huddling under the storm. I was a sparrow. She lifts me up. Here I am. I didn't disappear."

Ella smiles, shakes the woman's hand, and then glances the woods surrounding her home.

"That was unquestionably a unique story," Ella comments.

"Well, it was strange," she adds.

"Certainly nice meeting you."

Ella sighs in a tired manner. She is; however, glad to receive an unexpected visitor. The woman leans toward her dog and scratches its ears.

"We both enjoyed chatting with you," the woman replies.

"Hope to see you around, maybe. I live back that way there. Well, good-bye. Bye for now."

Ella lifts her arm and waves:

"Bye. Bye," she says.

"Where have I seen her before?" Ella whispers to herself.

"She looks familiar."

MONTHS LATER, EVENING FALLS on a summer night. Ella relaxes in bed. She stretches and cuddles into mountains of cotton and synthetic fibers of sheets. She bundles herself in a thick-blue blanket with threadbare satin trim – not her favorite, but comfortable nevertheless. Her thoughts are deep as she closes her eyes.

If you are a ghost, you won't notice the shadows casting elongated shapes from one window to the next, across the walls and ceiling. Ghosts experience our world like the scenes of their pasts. So you will have to dream up something else to be. Flies and moths are okay – but I would choose to be a cat for the moment. They are intuitive creatures and sensitive to everything about them. The shadows on Ella's walls appear as old alien friends, and for certain, they equally inspire a sleepy mind of a human or the skittish imagination of a cat.

Like a roller coaster ride temporarily forcing Ella's head into the hands of gravity and fast, predictable motion, the back of her head sinks into a pillow. She blows a deep, long breath and sighs.

A dream encourages gentle peace. This is what she sees: A miasma of mist and vapor. It imbues air like cottony clouds. It is continuous by miles wide and miles tall. Unmistakable luminance. Young birds prod and nestle mothers' feathery wings like puppies scratching noses against weedy turf.

Snuggle sounds secure these hours like cradles of angels' arms for all newborns of humankind and all life forms in between. Ella's feet find passage around cracked acorn shells and minuscule pieces of quartz and granite. She walks with a sixth sense around such things.

She is like a Native American Indian 200 years ago – stepping with careful purpose. She steps in the sense of a ghost who does not know of its own passing until the sun rising with angels, lined along its corridors beckons it home.

Tree frogs swim in nearby ponds. Shadowy branches and vines twist along paths of deer grazing in the camouflage of pearly luminosity. Thick clouds glide across the moon as shadows stretch against the lofty-bend of broom straw. Clustered rabbit's tobacco disappears into fog.

Possums and weasels run toward the local chicken plant that turns portions of a nearby town into Stinkville. Ella's feet brush the dewy ground through a steady and slow gait towards the deer. Ella raises a flashlight. Corn and rabbit food roll like miniature beads of gray iron through yellow oil from palm and fingers to the ground. Gentle chewing ceases and seeks to discern what she is. What does she want? Why is she here? What will she do?

It is at exactly forty winks from a rooster's call.

"Retrace your steps," Ella's mind warns.

"Retrace your steps!"

A foggy steam dissipates as the sun rises. Ella is still sleeping in soft, warm covers that garland her like a papoose. Loose and hard corn is scattered about the floor. You might wonder why that is there? I certainly do!

Spirit and Soul sit on either side of Ella's bed. Soul, dressed as if he's been on hiking and fishing trips, wears a hat with an abundance of fishing lures. Spirit, dressed in a long nightshirt and nightcap, holds a candle.

"Here we are!" Spirit says.

"In this glorious universe of stars and planets, the greens and blues of Mother Nature, her children of every life form and the misfits of maladjusted housekeepers who run between beauty and Hades making us miserable. Ella ignores them to survive," he continues.

"Well, thank you for that little speech," Soul replies.

"She's awake now. Did you happen to notice?"

Spirit breathes a sigh of acknowledgement.

"Yes," he answers.

"I did. Now, why don't you shower and spray before she notices you!"

Soul looks down and breathes in as if to check for offensive odor. Outside deer scatter like Cinderella racing the clock and traveling into shadowy leafless branches.

If by now you are a little tired of watching another person sleep while you observe her dream, have a sit. I claim the most comfortable green velvet chair next to the window. You can sit anywhere else – just not on Ella's bed. You see over across the room Soul and Spirit are very concerned about Ella.

Although still sleeping, Ella is thinking. She wonders if spirits of those lost in long ago wars ride on deer back as they race away. They appear to wave as if to say:

"Get up! Get going! We've made a path for you!"

Oh my goodness! Ella is opening her eyes. I caution you not to make one sound – not because she might hear you. She obviously cannot. It's not possible, nor is it allowed. I need my concentration to relay this story. Nevertheless, I can assure you my concentration is of great concern to me as I have had a baby holding onto my head and neck the past hour. You must admit this is a difficult task while taking you on this journey. I've obviously got your attention because I'm more than halfway through.

You know that Soul and Spirit are never aware of my presence or yours for that matter, and if you have forgotten, this is just a reminder. They certainly have the ability to occasionally glimpse small demons escorting housekeepers with ill and concealed intentions. All the same, we really should be careful just in case. One never knows when such rules might change.

"Did you say something?" Soul asks.

That was indeed a close call. Did you notice Soul nearly ease dropping on our conversation?

IT IS NOW A summer day. Ella is writing about a yesterday afternoon. She sits in her bed propped by pillows with a pen in one hand and her journal opened flat against her abdomen.

> *"This is a reflection. I nap*
> *after a morning swim and*
> *soaking in a warm tub and*
> *showering. I nurse my baby.*
> *I drift into a dream."*

The dream escorts Ella to a door. Walls are white-cream colored. Rooms are large with white brick-like tile on the floors. The furnishings are white. Ella finds herself with her parents, children, a few relatives and a friend of her mother's – the one she is named in honor of.

This friend makes haste in a kitchen preparing platters of fruit. Ella is later offered fruit; it includes dried plums and prunes. Ella picks one up and places it into her mouth. (If you don't mind me saying so, prunes and plums on one platter seem to be a bit redundant. But what can I say – but the truth? It's what was being served in this dream! If you don't care for either, you can imagine bananas or grapes, but it won't be the same!)

To her right is a fireplace with a white-cream wall above it and a raised lettering for the word: *"Jamestown."* Ella has a difficult time discerning the word. She decides it says, *"Jamesplace"* because she can't understand why it should say, *"Jamestown!"* The letters are no more than three-inches high. They are raised and recessed at the same time in a rectangular-shaped indenture of the wall above a fireplace.

The entire time she is here, she is distracted by the urge to go to the restroom and worries about privacy. She avoids the restroom. She crosses, uncrosses and re-crosses her legs.

"You have a one-way ticket," Ella's friend remarks.

"But you can return home on another ticket anytime you wish."

Ella chews a bite of fruit as she listens. The friend places a fruit platter on a coffee table directly front of her. The friend, referring to the ticket says:

"It might cost you."

An American Indian chief sits next to Ella. He is tall and between ages fifty and seventy. He cries quietly. No one speaks. Ella wakes. She finishes her journal entry and closes the cover. She re-opens the journal and adds two sentences:

> *"This dream is about purification.*
> *The Indian chief is symbolic of*
> *a spiritual protector."*

Ella places her pen and journal on the table, stands and answers the door. On the front step is another prospect looking for work. Ella invites her in, sits and begins the interview.

"What sort of reading do you do?" she asks.

The prospect curiously glances a table, where a book titled: *"FATES OF DISHONEST HOUSEKEEPERS"* is placed. The interview continues.

The prospect is not hired, and Ella continues about her day with the business of keeping order to household and family matters. Later that day, night falls into its cloudy camouflage for the wildlife that comes out of every nook and cranny of surrounding forests.

The evening waxes and wanes like a candle battling the winds of a ceiling fan and too much melted wax. It's time to sleep again. Ella stares upward – glancing bedroom windows as light streams in from the moon. In Ella's mind, there is the sound of tapping. It grows louder and is distinguished as typing. Her restless exhaustion tugs like an old mule not wishing to be pulled in from rain.

Ella's eyes faint like a rocking, stranded ferry caught in the Irish Sea. She sees the face of a man. It is unknown to her. Perhaps, it is Hedgecroft's face? Well, it is. It travels across the ocean. It thrashes eastern shores of America. It searches for a reckoning of what must be put right. It travels through trees. It peeks in at those trampling virtuously and not so by any measure through the winds of time.

Ella's eyes suddenly open. A thought of something she has forgotten nudges her to *not* sleep. She closes her eyes, but she is still awake. She recalls sitting at her office desk absorbed in thought. Quite unexpectantly, a slight touch to her lower right leg startles her. She glances the direction to see what it might be – a fly tasting salt, or perspiration? To her utter shock and horror, there about her feet and the floor, is a pair of watchful eyes attached to the unthinkable grotesque slinkiness. Those of a snake are upon her.

This memory prompts Ella to sit up. Perspiration beads across her forehead and upper lip. Ella's mind races. Why would a snake be inside? She recalls every time she exits her home, she cannot abandon the feeling of watchful eyes.

As Ella fights for sleep, she finds herself on a road in Memory Lane called *"Snakey Trails."* She walks up the sidewalk to her home of recent years and days. As she walks, she finds herself stepping over fat, lethargic and exhausted snakes littered about the grounds as if left there by the wagonload from a recent rainstorm. As Ella enters the house and walks to the kitchen, she finds Hal sitting at the counter. She sits next to him, as if time had stood still.

"I can't recall my age – possibly seven or eight," she says as if picking up where she left off.

"It is night. Late. My father and brother converse. We are on our way home. We've been at my grandmother's home in the country. Directly ahead we spy a creature."

Ella continues to relay this story and describes an evening's drive on a country road in Richfield, North Carolina. During such time, they spy a rattlesnake heading toward a horse stable. Ella's father drives over it. Then, he backs over it. He repeats this until he knows for sure it's demobilized and incapable of striking. In more direct language, it's dead – spiritually floating in the steamy waters surrounding a state mental hospital.

Twain is there with Soul and Spirit steadying their balance to fish it out. Snakes are not allowed there – just alligators. But in the reality of the Richfield evening is an opened newspaper on the front seat. Ella's father gathers the snake into these papers as if it has just been thrown back like a fish from the steamy gassy waters of the underworld. He places it onto the backseat floor. Ella and her brother John move opposite.

Back on Snakey Trails, Ella says to Hal:

"Thus, a science lesson on reptiles. The snake is dissected, skinned and boiled the following day. Its rattle is removed. The bones are strung onto thick thread. These things make great props for 'Show and Tell' at school. When we move to a new home, the bones and rattle are lost."

After this conversation, Ella leaves Snakey Trails in haste. She soon finds she is no better off and is still tossing and turning about her bed. Then, she recalls a dream – a nightmare, actually. Web balconies sport hissing snakes in a webbed theatre shaped like a dome around Ella's bed. It is in the shape of a canopy. It locks the mattress like a lid. It blocks her from moving one inch!

As you might imagine such creatures as snakes and spiders normally live in the forests and the cold, dark, creepy, creaky cellars of Memory Lane! Now, they have grown tired of their abodes and have crept up walls, ladders, stairwells and down chimneys to visit Ella again. Of course, their memories are of Ella as a child. They have not met her as an adult.

Now, Ella as an adult stands on a side street of Snakey Trails called: *"Thirty-Plus Years Ago"* carefully observing spiders at work. They diligently construct this dome with balconies, where small snakes coil up to watch the show below. They hiss cackles. Ella thinks of her conversation with Hal on Snakey Trails.

"I wake," she says.

"Snakes litter my bed."

The largest snake, a thick dark one, coils up on Ella-the-child's stomach.

"I'm going to bite you!" it threatens.

Ella as an adult continues to stand on the sidelines. When she musters the courage, she steps away from the shadows to the webbed dome, which covers the bed. Of course, when she pulls at the web, her hands pass through it.

"Don't worry," she says to Ella-the-child.

"I'll save you."

But, of course, Ella-the-child cannot hear her.

Ella-the-child shakes her head back and forth in a fury.

"No! Mommy! Daddy! Help me!" she cries.

The light comes on. Snakes scurry away. Snakes disappear into crevices about Ella's childhood bedroom. Ella's father inquires as to what is the matter. Ella-the-child tells him of the snakes.

"They are hiding now," she says.

"Don't go. Don't turn off the light. They will come back if you turn off the light!"

Ella's father looks under the bed as Ella stands by the door.

"Turn off the lights now. Let's see if they come back," he says.

Ella turns off the light. The snakes do not return. Then, she turns the light on, walks to her bed and crawls in. Her father walks to the door and turns off the light.

"The snakes will not be back," he says.

By now, Ella-the-adult has walked outdoors to view this from an outside window. When the light goes out, she waits for the snakes to come back. She is equipped with an axe, hoe and a shovel. They don't return, so Ella-the-adult turns around and heads down a street called: *"Current Lane."* Instead, she finds Twain holds a poster that reads: *"Go back to Snakey Trails."* She shouts, *"Why?"* But he does not answer. He smiles and points. As she prepares to step precisely, she notices most all of the snakes on the sidewalk have disappeared. She walks into the house and finds Hal at the counter. He sips a cup of coffee, as if time had been standing motionless.

"Have you ever thought you had company when logic says you are alone?" she asks Hal.

"The past couple of days in my office – It's not like an ancestor's spirit guiding me in genealogical endeavors. It feels alien – like being watched by something."

Hal's eyes spark with crazy humor as he looks at Ella. He is do-dahing an alien sort of tune.

"When you get terrestrial, you are always a bit strange," he replies.

Then, before Ella can say a word, he is off entertaining himself.

"Who you call'in strange, boy? I say, I'm strange, and you kind of strange too," he says.

Without another word – Ella leaves Snakey Trails and heads up the street to *"Current Lane."* She breathes a deep breath and closes her eyes for one second in her exhaustion of having to walk so much. When she opens her eyes, she is sitting up in bed. Her mind makes a giant sweep of the past like a giant broom from a giant janitor's giant closet, and that's the giant truth.

Within moments of this, Ella finds herself standing on a road called: *"Stay Calm Lane."* She walks to the breezeway of her current abode. She carries a glass of water and chews a handful of raisins. A slight bumping sound directs her attentions toward the trashcans and a lid. Briefly, she entertains the idea that what she sees is a possible snake. Then, she convinces herself one would never venture so close to her home.

In her office over the garage, Ella is absorbed in the deep thoughts of genealogical research. Without the slightest anticipation, she feels a tickle on her leg and finds part of Medusa's mane staring up. Ella stands cautiously and takes one very guarded step to the left. Then, raising her right leg steps up into a chair. It wobbles and rolls as Ella imagines what could happen if she falls. She tries to steady it as she holds the edges of the desk, eyes the telephone and dials 911. A policewoman on the telephone says:

"This is the police department; go ahead. We have you on the line."

Ella's throat is tight.

"I . . . . I need . . . . uh . . . ." she stammers.

"Are you being robbed, mam?" the policewoman asks.

"No," Ella replies.

"There's a snuh, a snuh, a snake in my office. Snake. Ah, snake!"

Ella's voice reduces to a whisper. Her eyes are fixed on the reptile. Ella stands in the chair.

"I am sending someone now," the policewoman says.

"Can you get to the door? Mam? Are you there?"

Ella in nervous shock replies:

"I am standing in my chair, and the snuh . . . . snake, well, it's all over the floor. It's blocking the door. It's everywhere about the floor. I think, I think I'm going to be sick. I think I am going to throw up."

Ella ponders to herself:

"I am going to faint! If you do, you will be down on that floor with that snake!"

The policewoman asks,

"Are you away from the snake?"

Ella indicates 'yes' with affirmative sounds.

"Stay calm; an officer is on the way," the policewoman says.

"I am dispatching someone from Animal Control too."

An officer arrives and removes the snake – a veteran black snake nearly twelve feet long. A very unusual size it is too! This snake was attracted to a bird's nest resting atop an air conditioning unit. A window at the top of the stairs is temporarily removed. It rests against the wall outside the door of the office, waiting for repair.

The snake evidently smelled the bird's nest. In days past, it scurries up the brick wall of the back of the garage, enters through the open window space, crosses the small hall in front of the door, and then slithers through the threshold. This occurs on long stretches Ella leaves the door open while making trips to the house to refill her cup.

The snake twists and turns. The officer carries it down. When he reaches the foot of the stairs, he pops its head with a pole, rendering it to Never-to-Return Land of the Ever After.

Chapter 22

Medusa's Head, the Brown Sack & the Cold, Crusty-white of the Apocalypse

THE NEXT MORNING ELLA sits upright with her journal and pen and recounts details of another dream. In it, she races to the door. On the way, she grabs her brown jacket. She runs to the edge of the woods. Instead of holding a jacket in her hands, she finds it transforms into a large brown sack. As she opens it, the roar of a bear resonates to a jaguar's screeching.

A thick and sluggish king snake on the ground twists in peculiar curves and shapes as if in pain. With only this as a warning, small snakes pour from its gut. In the dirt, it looks like an abstract of Medusa's head.

Ella lifts and scoops each wiggling strand into the bag and ties the top closed. She throws it to the sky, where the wind snatches the bag and carries it to the ocean to another continent.

Ella closes her journal and goes about her day. That evening, she crawls into bed as she does most evenings and drifts to another dream. She travels to Australia and sees on the seashore a nameless stranger. It is a sunny day. The stranger notices something drifting in the waves and picks it up. It is an empty brown sack. The bystander, puzzled, examines the bag. A small green snake falls from it onto the sand.

As we all are prone to do, Ella travels from one dream to the next as if making up for lost time. Excursions no doubt grasp the attentions of Soul and Spirit.

Soul is dressed in plaid and tacky tourist clothes like what an outdated, carefree American might wear in Italy. Spirit, dressed in a large, white night shirt and nightcap, holds a lit lantern.

Soul and Spirit stand meekly next to one another. Both are slightly transparent – you can see some of the trees through them.

"Where are we off to now?" Soul asks.

"Your guess is as good, well. Hmm," Spirit answers.

Ella, thirsty from having walked miles across the Australian outback, looks up and finds a shimmering castle. Twain's spirit is there with his pants rolled three inches above his ankles. There are bunionectomy and hammertoe surgery scars on both of his feet.

"Well, hello my old friend," Twain says.

"What brings you here?" he asks.

"I need a vacation," Ella replies.

Ella enters the castle via a nun – doubling as a housekeeper. She climbs stairs to a balcony, sits in a lounge chair and removes her sunglasses. Soul rises from Ella's body for its reprieve and leaves Spirit just enough of itself to keep Ella breathing. It rises to the sky.

Days continue, and as you might expect, Ella drifts to sleep each night. On one particular night, her dream travels take her to snowy grounds of a medieval forest. She hikes in a forest with her uncle, some cousins and an aunt and stumbles upon a clearing.

Arranged like cemetery tombstones are three horse heads balanced on the earth's crust. They are white as if painted and plastered. Two appear exactly like life-size statues – motionless. The third one struggles and moves as if partially trapped.

Ella strokes its face and is perplexed as to how anyone would do such a thing. With each few seconds that pass, life in it becomes increasingly more apparent. It rocks as the earth cracks open suddenly exploding it into the air like a Trojan horse. Ella climbs onto its back and rides quickly through blue-white snow. Soul and Spirit observe with much interest.

The horse gallops away into purple dusk. As it returns, some ninety minutes before Ella's waking, Spirit initiates conversation with Soul.

Both Spirit and Soul, dressed head-to-toe in winter caps, coats, scarves and gloves, are cold to the point their cheeks and noses are red. As Ella and the horse race past them, a scroll drifts from the sky. As it lands in the snow, Spirit picks it up.

"Ninety minutes later," Spirit says reading the scroll.

"Well, that's assuring," he says.

"It's been ninety minutes. She won't have the slightest recollection."

Soul looks out into the snow as Spirit comments.

"I see you are well rested," he says.

"Devoid of negativity? I trust all is well for the present? . . . and the future?"

"Yes, and how is our Ella – you know, her mind?" Soul inquires.

"Well rested, and ready for a brand new day," Spirit answers.

Chapter 23

Rowing on . . .

THE NEXT MORNING SOUL and Spirit stand next to Ella's bed. They remove their gloves, hats, scarves and coats. A television voice is faintly heard.

"It's going to be sunny skies today," the television weather reporter says.

"High seventies, low eighties."

The morning sun rises. It lights windows near Ella's bed as she opens her eyes. Hal walks in. His feet shuffle across the floor. His toenails are now manicured, cut short. The large toe is wrapped in gauze. Hal places a cup of herb tea on the nightstand and walks to the window. Looking out, he places his palms against the windowsill. He leans through the window.

"Have you noticed our garden lately?" he asks Ella.

Ella stands and walks to the window, glances the garden abundant with everything green and beautiful and inhales fresh air. As she exhales, the wind blows.

Now, if you will, glance overtop of Ella. Notice there on the ground beneath the window is a harmless green snake. Oh well. That's enough for now.

P.S.: Are you familiar with the nursery rhyme, *"Row, row, row your boat?"*

Here's my version of it:

Row. Row. Row your life gently
through your dreams, merrily, merrily,
merrily, merrily life is full of streams.

THE END . . . for now anyway.

Bon appétit, bon voyage, au revoir, bonne chance, bonsoir et bon ménage!

For Your Information

A S YOU MIGHT HAVE guessed, the story you have just read was influenced by a hodgepodge of things and people in my life and by an assortment of places I have visited.

❖ CAMILLE CLAUDEL is mentioned in *Chapter 2* of this story. Camille (born: December 8th, 1864; passed away: October 19th, 1943) was a daughter of Louise-Athanaïse Cerveaux and Louis-Prosper Claudel, of a town called Fère in the province of Tardenois (Aisne), France. Her siblings were Paul, a poet and Louise. The father of Camille's mother was a doctor who worked in Fère. Camille's father was a registrar of mortgages in Fère. Camille was an artist who was best known for sculpting. Some of her sculptures include: a bronze bust called, *"Psalm,"* (1889); a bronze bust of *"Rodin,"* (1892), a bronze bust: *"Giganti,"* (1885); a terra cotta bust of Louise Claudel (1885), a marble bust titled: *"The Little Chatelaine,"* (1896); a sculpture in onyx and bronze titled: *"The Gossipers,"* (1897) and many more.

❖ WILLIAM MILLER (1810-1872), a Scottish Victorian poet, wrote in 1841 a Scottish nursery rhyme titled: *"Wee Willie Winkie."* He is mentioned in *Chapter 9* of this story.

The Scottish version is rough enough! I can't say I've mastered the dialects, accents and language of Scotland, but it begins like this:

Wee Willie Winkie runs through the toun,
Up stairs and doon stairs in his nicht-goun,
Tirlin' at the window, cryin' at the lock,
"Are the weans in their bed, for it's noo ten
o'clock?"

Skipping over the middle stanzas to the last one, it reads:

Wearit is the mither that has a stoorie wean,
A wee stumple stoussie, that canna rin his lane,
That has a battle aye wi' sleep before he'll close an
ee
But a kiss frae aff his rosy lips gi'es strength anew
tae me.

For the rest of us illiterates of Scottish poetry, here is a nice translation of those two stanzas.

Wee Willie Winkie runs through the town,
Up stairs and down stairs in his night-gown,
Tapping at the window, crying at the lock,
"Are the children in their bed, for it's now ten
o'clock?"
. . . .
Weary is the mother who has a dusty child,
A small short child, who can't run on his own,
Who always has a battle with sleep before he'll close
an eye
But a kiss from his rosy lips gives strength anew to
me.

William Miller, born in Glasgow, lived at #4 Ark Lane in Dennistoun, Scotland. Although he is said to have been a carpenter, he was also a poet and songwriter. Some of his works were published in magazines and as a collection titled: *"Whistle-binkie: Stories for the Fireside."* (1842). He passed away without a cent. His remains are buried in a family plot in Tollcross Cemetery, Glasgow.

❖ IF YOU ARE FAMILIAR with the French language you probably know of the words *"vraiment"* and *"vrai."* Together as *"vraiment, vrai,"* they mean *"really true."* Can you find a clue in a character's name with a similar sound? I put this character's name in as a secret symbol in *Chapter 11.* Of course, if you find it, it won't be a secret anymore!

❖ DID YOU KNOW THAT throwing salt over your shoulder is a task one does for good luck or for superstitious reasons? If you noticed in *Chapter 12,* I did this before beginning *Chapter 13.* I am not really superstitious about the number 13. People who have a real fear of this number have what is called: *"triskaidekaphobia."* The number 13 got a bad reputation because Judas, one of Jesus' disciples, was the 13th to sit at the table of The Last Supper. Because of this, some believe the number carries a curse. For others the number 13 is considered a strange number – not only because it is an odd number – one more than 12, but also because the lunisolar calendar had 13 months every second or third year. The Gregorian (the most widely used calendar in the world and modeled after the Julian calendar) and Lunar Islamic calendars always have 12 months in a year. The Gregorian calendar was decreed by Pope Gregory XIII (the 13th!!! – pass the salt, please). It was named for him. The years in this calendar are numbered from the traditional birth year of Jesus. This is called the Anno Domini (A.D.) era, or Common Era or Common Christian Era. Just for your information, you might be curious to know that the specific fear of Friday the 13th is called: *"paraskavedekatriaphobia"* and also *"friggatriskaidekaphobia."* If you want to know more about such things, refer to encyclopedias, dictionaries, reference books or a doctor.

How many times can you guess the number 13 or thirteen is mentioned throughout this book? If you guessed 13, you are correct – minus the *Table of Contents* page, which makes 14.

❖ AUGUSTE RODIN (born November 12th, 1840 as François-Auguste-René Rodin; passed away: November 17th, 1917), son of Marie Cheffer and Jean-Baptiste Rodin, a police department clerk. His sister was Maria. His wife was Rose Beuret. Beuret and Rodin had a son: Auguste-Eugène Beuret (1866-1934). Auguste Rodin, an artist, is best known for sculpting. Some of my favorite sculptures by Rodin include: *"Thought,"* (1893-95); *"The Thinker"* (at first called *"Dante,"* in the early 1880s). Of course, like the works of Camille, Rodin's works are numerous. Rodin is mentioned in *Chapter 14.*

❖ FAUGH-A-BALLAGH IS an old Irish war chant. (This term is used in *Chapter 19.*) It was used by the Irish Brigade in the Civil War in the War Between the States – the North and South of the United States [1861-1865]. The Irish Brigade was a unit of the Union Army commanded by Brigadier General Thomas Meagher. The Irish Brigade fought Sept. 17th, 1862 at Antietam in Maryland; 23,000 men were killed, wounded or missing. The Irish Brigade shouted *"Faugh-a-Ballagh"* as they marched into battle. The brigade was made up of Irish immigrants to New York at the time. They marched in carrying a green battle flag and were joined by others not of Irish origin or descent.

❖ AUSTRALIA HAS MORE THAN 100 different species of venomous snakes, but approximately one-fifth of these can kill humans. Australia, the only continent where venomous snakes outnumber non-venomous snakes, is home to non-venomous snakes such as carpet snakes, files snakes and several species of constricting python. The longest is said to be the amethystine – also called a rock python. Its average length is 11.5 feet; however, it can reach 28 feet long. Most dangerous snakes in Australia include: brown snakes, mulga, tiger snakes, the king brown snake, death adders, red-bellied black snakes and taipans. Venom in an inland taipan can kill 100,000 mice. Inland taipans are one of the world's most deadly snakes. (Australia is mentioned in *Chapter 22.*)

THE END

© Copyright 2007 by Hélène Andorre Hinson Staley and Metallo House Publishers.